Love and Murder

Love and Murder

PETER WHALLEY

A CRIME CLUB BOOK
DOUBLEDAY
NEW YORK LONDON TORONTO SYDNEY AUCKLAND

A CRIME CLUB BOOK
PUBLISHED BY DOUBLEDAY
a division of Bantam Doubleday Dell Publishing Group, Inc.
666 Fifth Avenue, New York, New York 10103

DOUBLEDAY and the portrayal of a man with a gun
are trademarks of Doubleday, a division of
Bantam Doubleday Dell Publishing Group, Inc.

Library of Congress Cataloging-in-Publication-Data
Whalley, Peter, 1946–
Love and murder.
"A Crime Club book."
I. Title.
PR6073.H35L68   1989   823'.914   88-33560

ISBN 0-385-24853-9
Copyright © 1985 by Peter Whalley
ALL RIGHTS RESERVED
PRINTED IN THE UNITED STATES OF AMERICA
JULY 1989
OG

For Ruth—With love

"See how love and murder will out."
—Congreve
The Double Dealer

"Only connect."
—Forster
Howards End

Love and Murder

I

Pavan Singh Sambhi was born in 1921 in the town of Jullundur in Northern India. He was born also into the minority religious sect of Sikhism. It was a sect which instructed him, among other things, that his hair should remain forever uncut and be covered by a turban.

After a rudimentary education at the local Gurdwara—the Sikh temple—he went to work at the age of nine in his father's small textile business, then, eleven years later, married a wife who had been chosen for him and whose chastity was beyond doubt. The occupying British forces were viewed by Pavan Singh Sambhi with respect and gratitude. They were the temporal expression of the Divine Will, imposing order and justice upon what would be chaos without them. Besides which, they were good customers for his father's cloth.

Then, in 1947, India achieved independence, the British made an orderly withdrawal and, after a few weeks of uneasy calm, the feared maelstrom began. The Punjab, now artificially divided by the new border with Pakistan, was swept by religious and tribal wars as the distrust of centuries was given full rein. There were religion-inspired riots in the nearby towns of Amritsar and Hoshiarpur, after which the Sutlej River, a tributary of the Indus, was stained pink and carried an uncountable number of bloated bodies along it.

It was an omen that Pavan Singh Sambhi was not slow to take. He must flee the advancing slaughter in search of the security he had once known. In September 1948 he brought his wife to England and settled in Southall in the East End of London.

It was a cultural shock for which he could hardly have been prepared. In place of the fanaticism he'd left, he found a nation on the make. Spirituality seemed totally absent; having a good time was what mattered and never mind how. It was difficult to believe that those well-disciplined regiments of the British Army in India had come from these tightly packed streets with their pubs and chip shops.

He felt himself an alien and turned even more fervently to the teachings of Sikhism. More than anything, he strove to ensure that his two daughters, Nishi and Shina, remained untainted by the promiscuity and immorality of their host country. Nishi was submissive and accepted without a murmur her parents' instructions on dress and behaviour and seemed as pleased as they were when it was arranged that she should marry a young Sikh doctor whose caste and family background were on a par with her own. The wedding was in August, 1980, at the Southall Gurdwara with, afterwards, a reception for seventy at the Post House Hotel in Ilford.

"My dear," said Pavan Singh Sambhi to his wife, "half our task is over. With God's help, we will now complete it."

But Shina, the other half of the task, was not the placid and obedient Nishi. As younger daughter, she had enjoyed small freedoms denied her elder sister, freedoms that had only fed her dissatisfaction with the family lifestyle. Why shouldn't she talk to the boys with whom she went to school—particularly when they seemed so eager to talk to her? Why not wear fashionable clothes —never mind that they weren't always loose fitting and seemed designed to reveal rather than conceal the female form?

With Nishi now married, Shina received her parents' undivided attention. There were nightly rows as she struggled against their attempts to discipline her.

Finally, in December 1982, at the age of nineteen, she left home. She had no job and little money but she was an attractive and spirited girl and was in no doubt she would survive. The curses of her father rang in her ears and her mother wept as she closed the family door behind her and headed for the tube.

Frith Street was close to the heart of Soho, London's square mile of sleazy sex just north of the statue of Eros in Piccadilly Circus. Like everywhere in Soho, it was a curious cheek-by-jowl mixture of the legitimate and the dubious. There was a Greek coffee shop, two restaurants, a newsagent's and a confectioner's as well as blocks of anonymous office accommodation. There were also two sex shops, a nude encounter parlour and three cinema clubs, one of which specialised in gay movies. A number of open doorways had handwritten signs urging the caller to climb the thinly carpeted stairs to where "Melinda" or "Jade" or "New Young French Model" was in attendance.

And there was a strip club. Just the one, since such places had been in decline since the mushrooming of the porno cinemas, and then the peep shows and encounter parlours. In the sex industry, as in the rag trade, fashions came and went.

But the City Strip had survived them, a basement club catering to tourists and businessmen with none of the "champagne" at fifty pounds a bottle or the "hostesses" at a hundred a night that were the norm in other, flashier clubs. Five rows of old cinema seats looked onto a small stage; a young man sat behind a one-way mirror, operating the lighting, the curtains and the music.

It was here that Shina Sambhi had found work. Six times a day, under the stage name of Charmain, she performed her routine, removing a few flimsy garments and then simulating masturbation. It seemed a harmless and easy way of earning money, as well as signalling in no uncertain terms her rejection of Sikhism.

The main entrance to the club, through which the punters came, displayed photographs of the artistes around a pay booth. A notice assured that there would be no further charges when once inside.

A few yards further along was a small alleyway, leading nowhere and littered with old rubbish. Halfway down was a door marked Private. Behind this, a flight of stairs led directly to the side of the stage below. It was by this route that the girls came and went. They already wore their costumes under their outdoor clothes and thus could turn up on stage, perform, and be away again within minutes.

Tuesday, July 23 was sunny and cloudless, another day in what was already being dubbed Britain's long, hot summer. The daytime temperature had been in the upper seventies for the past three weeks, and there were already predictions of water shortages.

At 1:35 P.M. a tall, thin man in his early twenties with ginger hair and a moustache and a small scar to the side of his left eye came out of the Tottenham Court Road underground station, crossed Soho Square and entered Frith Street. He was casually dressed out of deference to the weather, but the moccasin shoes, the slacks and the short-sleeved shirt he was wearing had all been recently purchased and had cost good money. He was carrying a briefcase.

He passed the entrance to City Strip without giving it so much as a glance, then turned abruptly into the alleyway alongside it. Stepping over the rubbish, he went along until he reached the door marked Private, where he stopped and stood listening. From below came the faint sound of Elkie Brooks singing "Warm and Tender Love."

On stage, Charmain was almost halfway through her routine. She was standing with her back to the audience and was naked but for a sequined G-string. This she undid slowly, then let fall to the ground. She lifted her arms and swayed—more or less in time to the music—before turning one-hundred-and-eighty degrees.

There was an air of solemnity among her audience as they concentrated their eyes upon her crotch. The tape slid from Elkie Brooks to Bette Midler singing "La Vie en Rose."

It was Charmain's cue to go into the second half of her routine. She dropped into a sitting position and slowly spread her legs. She stroked the inside of one brown thigh, then the inside of the other.

There was an instant when she was aware of something coming down the steps at the side of the stage, then a smash of glass and a smell of petrol. The next moment a sheet of orange flame had flung itself across half the stage and was rolling towards her.

A verse from the *Adi Granth*, the sacred writings of Sikhism, came to her.

The Universe is burning
Be merciful O God.

II

There was water, translucent and quivering with sunlight, above, below and all around him. He'd lost all sense of how far he was below the surface and was conscious only of a fierce dread that he might never escape, as well as relief that his left hand was still clenched tightly around the arm of the small girl.

He kicked with his feet and paddled as best he could with his other free arm and finally felt the both of them rising. Though not far enough. Panic came to him as the surface stayed tantalisingly beyond his reach. He was still imprisoned in this empty world of water, silent but for a muffled thrashing sound that was his own kicking and clawing. They must have gone deeper than he'd realised. His head began to throb and his chest ached, then the bright surface was dancing inches before his eyes. Another final heave and he broke it, thrusting his head out into sunlight and noise.

He still had hold of the girl. There were shouts from far away but he was deafened by his own greedy, desperate gasping for breath and couldn't hear them. He pushed himself backwards, kicking with his feet, and then, with a mighty effort, hauled the inert body of the girl on top of him in a crude approximation to the life-saving method he'd once been taught.

His head slipped again beneath the surface, but he'd glimpsed the shore and struck out for it. He had the girl's head lodged against his chest with her small body trailing like seaweed below him. He coughed from the water he'd taken in and tried to regulate his breathing but knew there was a limit to how long he could continue. He was already exhausted. There was an awful and growing temptation to just give up and allow them both to return to that watery limbo. The shore seemed no nearer.

"Here!"

"Hang on!"

This time he heard the shouts of encouragement. Heard, too, the creaking of wood and then saw the shape of a rowing boat coming from behind him. For a moment it seemed certain to run him down—he could do nothing, was too weak to avoid it—but then hands were fending him off. Someone cried, "I've got her! I've got her!" and he realised he had to let go of the girl.

Released from his burden, he was able to reach up for the side of the boat. But it was too high, bulging out above him. Or he was too weak.

He began to sink again, but now there were other hands coming from the boat that grasped his. He resurfaced to see the anxious, eager faces of strangers looking down at him.

"We've got you."

"You're all right."

They seemed to understand that he'd never manage to climb aboard and was too heavy for them to lift into that small boat, and so held him where he was, in the water. An oar began to move, cautiously, being careful to avoid him, on his side of the boat. He felt himself being towed along.

The shouting from the bank approached. He saw the crowd that had come together, and then his feet were scraping and bumping along the bed of the lake.

" 'S all right," he spluttered, trying to make them let go of his hands. "I can . . ." But the word "stand" was lost as he coughed and retched.

"He can stand," somebody said, and they let go of his arms.

For a second he could stand but do nothing else—his legs wouldn't move—and he watched the boat going away from him. Then its wake tugged at his body and pulled him into a forward stumble. The water level fell to his chest, freeing his arms. The bed of the lake rose, the water dropped abruptly away, he stumbled onto the shore and collapsed forward onto his hands and knees.

He puked a thin mixture of lake water and then rolled onto his back and lay there, the blood beating in his ears and the sun strong on his face.

A few yards to his right the commotion that had greeted the boat's return was now hushed as the fight was on for the life of the young girl. Someone was giving her the kiss of life. Then there was a cry—"She's breathing!"—and a concerted wail of delight and relief.

She's alive, thought Martyn. Good. He hadn't yet the energy to do more than simply record the thought—she was alive—it hadn't all been a waste of time.

With the girl out of danger, there was opportunity now for him to receive his due share of attention. People detached themselves from the group around her and came to stand and stare down at him.

"You all right?"

"You did a great job. Well done."

He smiled weakly and nodded, wanting not honour and glory but to be left alone.

An elderly military-looking man in khaki shorts offered his hand.

"That was a very courageous thing you did, young man. I think you deserve the highest praise."

Not wanting to appear discourteous, Martyn somehow found the strength to lever himself up onto his elbows and take the proffered hand. "Thanks," he muttered. Though his actions seemed to him to have been as much instinctive as courageous.

He'd been there on the shore, looking after the rowing boats and gazing idly across the lake, when suddenly there'd been a wave and a scream from far out. He'd flung himself into the water and headed for the spot which, by the time he got to it, was marked only by ever-widening ripples. He'd taken a breath and dived—and in the quiet, clear world had seen the spread-eagled body of a young girl floating gently downwards.

He'd forced himself towards her, made a grab at an out-stretched arm, and then had come the fight to get both of them back to the shore.

"Here. You look as though you could use this."

It was a silver hip flask, being thrust at him by a woman's hand.

"No . . ." he started to say, but she'd have none of it and made him take it.

"It won't do you any harm. You must have already taken enough water to go with it."

He smiled at the joke, unscrewed the top and took a sip. It was whisky. "Go on . . . !" she urged, and he took some more.

He also took a look at her and saw a blonde who was quite tall
and probably in her early thirties—anyway, a few years older than
he was. She had even features, heavily tanned, and a slim figure
beneath her jeans and tee-shirt that was already distracting some
of the bystanders away from Martyn.

"Thanks," he said, and returned the flask.

She dropped to her haunches beside him.

"Well, you seem to be quite the hero."

"Not really."

"What's your name?"

It struck him as an oddly direct question, but he hadn't yet the
strength to do other than answer it.

"Martyn. Martyn Culley." Then, worried by the possibility,
"You're not a reporter or anything, are you?"

She laughed. "Not anything. I live here."

A youngish couple in beachwear but with a distressed air about
them that commanded attention appeared before him.

"We're Amanda's parents," said the man. "The girl you saved.
We're her parents."

"Oh . . . right," said Martyn, and got shakily to his feet.

"I . . . well, we just wanted to say . . ."

"You saved her life," said his wife tearfully. "We'll never forget
that. You saved her life."

"I just hope she's all right," said Martyn, embarrassed for
them, aware of the massive debt they must feel but could never
repay.

The husband held out his hand. "You were marvellous. Bloody
marvellous." And tears began to roll down his cheeks.

They shook hands solemnly before the arrival of an ambulance
gave the couple their cue to hurry away. Relieved to see them go,
Martyn waved farewell, then turned to find that the woman who'd
offered him the hip flask was still there beside him.

"And what do you do when you're not saving lives?"

"Not a lot," he said, happy to get back to casual chat after the
emotionally charged encounter with Amanda's parents. "I'm in
charge of these rowing boats."

There were twelve of them altogether, the majority still lying
there on the shore, drawn up in a line beyond the water's edge.

He gave an apologetic shrug. "It's not exactly the most demanding job in the world."

"No," she agreed. "So why do it?"

"Well . . . I sort of got stranded here. And there are worse ways of spending the summer."

"Do you smoke?"

He said he didn't, so she lit a cigarette for herself and made him explain what he'd meant by his talk about being "stranded."

Accustomed now to obeying her, he told of how he had left university with a near-useless degree in philosophy and for the past four years had bummed his way around the country working as labourer, hot dog seller, fruit picker, gardener and odd-job man before finally landing the respectable post of theatre administrator. Unfortunately the theatre in question had been a tiny outfit operating on a shoestring and from the back of a Transit van. The company of five had come together in April and built a repertoire that had included Noël Coward, Tom Stoppard and an improvised play on the life and work of William Wordsworth. They then embarked on what should have been a four-month tour of the Lake District, playing in pubs, clubs and village halls.

Martyn's job was to drive the van, load and unload the scenery and listen to everybody slagging off everybody else.

"That's an administrator . . . ?" exclaimed the woman, highly entertained.

"Not really." He gave a rueful smile. "What it was was a job."

"So what happened?"

"Oh, there was a lot of aggro flying around. Then one of the actresses left. I mean just upped and went. And we had a meeting and decided to pack the whole thing in. I think everybody was relieved, tell you the truth."

"And how did you come by the rowing boats?"

"Oh, they're not mine. I was going to hitch back down south, and then the man who owns them asked me if I wanted a job for the summer. There was accommodation went with it so . . ." He shrugged. Here he was.

"A man for all seasons," she said.

He laughed. Then noticed a stocky grey-haired man hurrying towards them. "Talk of the devil . . ." he muttered.

"Martyn," barked the grey-haired man as he approached,

"Martyn, what the hell's been going on? Somebody was saying about a kid . . . ?"

"There was a girl nearly drowned," explained Martyn. "But I think she's going to be all right."

"What, she fell out of one of the boats?"

"No. She was swimming."

"Ah. Well, that's all right then."

"It's all right because Martyn saved her," said the woman sharply. "That's the only reason it's all right."

The grey-haired man looked at her, taken aback by the implied rebuke. "Oh. Did he. Well."

"Though I can understand you're relieved there won't be any insurance claim for you to worry about."

The sarcasm turned him red in the face. He opened his mouth to reply but met her level gaze and turned instead to Martyn.

"And are you all right? I mean you can carry on here for the rest of the day, can you?"

"Yes," said Martyn. "I'm OK, Mr. Hutton, don't worry."

"I'm glad to hear it," said Mr. Hutton. He gave a hostile glance at the woman, then stamped back to where he had left his car.

"Charming. He thinks that he owns you as well as the boats."

"Me, the boats, two ice cream vans and a café," grinned Martyn. At least there was no danger of Joe Hutton lauding him as a hero, a rare point in his favour.

Then, despite the sun and the whisky, Martyn gave an involuntary shiver.

"You need to keep warm," she said, observing him.

"I'm OK, just . . . nothing." And he shivered again.

"Of course you are," she said tartly. "Nothing more serious than pneumonia. Wait there."

And, before he could protest, she'd jogged away through the trees and towards the car park behind them.

Martyn felt annoyed with himself and a touch foolish. He'd always reckoned he kept himself in good shape, yet was now standing shivering and shaking after a two-minute dip on a hot day. Perhaps he'd come nearer to death than he'd thought.

She returned with a tartan car rug that she insisted on draping around him.

"It's very kind of you," he said. "I mean, the whisky and everything."

He was conscious now of how mindlessly he'd prattled on about himself, not even asking her name.

"Yeah well, you caught me on a good day," she said dismissively and glanced at her watch. "Look, I've got to go. See you keep warm, OK?"

"Yes," he said, and started to remove the rug, but she pushed it back across his shoulders.

"You hang on to that. You can give it back next time you see me."

"But suppose . . ."

"You will. Don't worry."

"What's your name?" he asked hurriedly as she started to move away.

"Julie," she said. "Bye."

He watched her go through the trees and get into what looked like a Porsche, though he couldn't be sure at that distance.

"Bye," he called after her.

The lake shore around him had settled back to its customary summer calm with families picnicking and the odd hopeful fisherman. Beside the rowing boats on the shore, there were two that would be out for another half hour and the one that had been used in the rescue and then left half in and half out of the water.

Martyn hauled it up the shingle until it was in line with the others. Then he went and sat in his usual spot, which gave him the base of a tree as a backrest and where he found the book he'd dropped so hurriedly before his rush into the water.

Though it was some time before he fell to reading again. Instead, he sat with the rug drawn tightly about him and gazed across Coniston Water. From his position on the north shore, he could take in the full five-mile length of it, with the massed trees of Grizedale Forest rising to his left and the uncompromising humps of Coniston Fells and the Old Man of Coniston to his right.

The lake waters were so still as to mirror accurately the heights around them. It was an image that made him uncomfortably aware of a terrain below that surface that could be even more dangerous than the fells that surrounded it.

III

The waiter left the bar with a tray of drinks, crossed the club and came to a table which was cleverly sited so as to afford complete privacy while giving a view of everyone else's comings and goings. Sprawled around the table at the moment were three men— Arnie Bish, Phil Cavanaugh and Ginger Morrisey. All three were full-time, lifelong villains and, outside of a court of law, would have been proud to admit to the description.

The first drink, a scotch and soda, was for Arnie Bish, since it was Arnie who owned the club as well as much else besides. He was in his middle forties with a fast receding hairline but radiated a compelling and even youthful energy in his eager scrutiny of the world around him.

"Cheers, John," he said, taking the drink.

The waiter, who was called Paul, gave a small bow of the head and took the second drink, which was bourbon on the rocks, from his tray. This was for the man to Arnie Bish's right, a man perhaps ten years his junior and fifty pounds heavier, christened Kevin Morrisey but fated to be known as Ginger by the hair on his head and the blotches of freckles that covered his face and the backs of his hands.

The remaining pint of lager was for Phil Cavanaugh, another big man but running to fat with a thick neck and podgy features. The oldest of the three, Cavanaugh was a long-standing crony of Arnie Bish, originally a meat porter who'd risen on Arnie's coat-tails till he was now right-hand man in a small empire. Morrisey, on the other hand, had joined the firm only eighteen months earlier, fresh from working as troubleshooter for Lionel Trilling, a bookie with a chain of shops and a lot of enemies. These Morrisey had ably dealt with; it was a heart attack that had done for Lionel and left Morrisey unemployed.

"This weather, eh," said Cavanaugh, and took a long pull at his lager. "Never known anything like it."

The waiter retreated to the body of the club. There was a pause during which Ginger Morrisey lit a cigarette.

"All right then," said Arnie Bish. "Tell us about the fire."

It was Cavanaugh who replied.

"Fair amount of damage. But apparently nothing structural."

"It's not going to fall down?"

"Not unless we want it to."

There was an appreciative chuckle, then Arnie said, "Go on."

"Well, obviously the club had to close. At least for a week or two, for redecoration and whatnot. Then back to normal or whatever you like."

"What about the Old Bill, what're they doing?"

"Not a lot, so far as I'm aware." He turned to Ginger Morrisey for confirmation and got it with a nod of the head. Encouraged, he went on, "I think they're sort of, you know, waiting to see whether it's just a one-off. Or the start of something."

"Yeah," said Arnie. "That's what I was wondering as well."

"But I mean there was nobody hurt. I mean no members of the public. Only the girl got a bit burnt, that was all."

"Which bit?" asked Ginger, and they all laughed.

An Atlas of the Underworld, were there such a publication, would have outlined the territories of fifteen or sixteen different "firms" that, among them, accounted for the major part of the capital's organised crime. George Sempers in South London, the Fermani brothers from the East End, Billy Ridley, born in Notting Hill but now with interests in Camberwell and Deptford, the Carrs, father and sons, from North London, Francis Kelly, who had drinking clubs in Ealing and Acton, Billy "the Kid" Marshall (Fulham and Wandsworth), Harvey Phillips (Camden Town), the West Indians from Notting Hill, currently leaderless since Andrew "Sugarboy" Lewis overdosed himself, Joey Lubin (Battersea), Alex McLoughlin (East End) . . . and the rest.

Each held their own territory, as clearly defined and as scrupulously honoured as that of any Borough Council. Most were into sex, video piracy, gambling and protection. Some had more esoteric sidelines such as drugs or forgery. All had diversified to a greater or lesser extent into legitimate businesses, usually pubs, betting shops, amusement arcades or launderettes.

It was a far cry from the fifties and sixties when London had been dominated by only two or three firms, intent on annihilating one another. At the head of the postwar villains had been the Messina brothers, George Caruana and, the biggest of them all, Billy Hill. Then had come the Krays, the Richardsons and the Tibbs, whose rivalries with one another and with other, lesser contenders had often left the West End looking like a battle-ground. The normal police view of all this mayhem—that it was all right so long as the villains were chopping down one another —was given a jolt by the public outcry that followed the Great Train Robbery of 1963. Political pressure forced them into aban-doning the laissez-faire of old and led finally to the Richardsons being put away in '67 and then, bigger fish still, the Krays in '68.

It was the beginning of relative peace with a new breed of villains who weren't necessarily out to rule the entire world—just their own particular neck of it.

However, like their bloodier ancestors before them, the new gang lords marked their graduation into the big time by estab-lishing themselves in premises of their own somewhere within the square mile of Soho. These were usually drinking clubs but served also as headquarters and embassies—a base from which they could operate in safety and comfort while keeping their ears close to the common ground all of them nervously shared.

Arnie Bish was one such firm. Not one of the largest but se-curely based in prostitution, videos and protection—steady, reli-able incomes that avoided the sudden police interest that, say, drugs occasionally attracted.

Arnie had grown up in Bethnal Green, as good a place to learn the ropes as any. Like many of his friends, he'd indulged in petty theft; unlike them, he'd been caught, ended up in Borstal and thus had his card marked for life. He returned to the Green, dabbled in protection and ran a whorehouse in nearby Islington, modest enough operations for a man with Arnie's ambitions.

Then in May 1974, he went for broke, leading a couple of mates who had the bottle for it (one of whom was Phil Cava-naugh) in two daring robberies, both of which succeeded. The first was a daylight raid on Barclays Bank in Edmonton. Two of them went in with stocking masks over their faces and sawn-off shotguns in their hands while the third waited outside in a stolen Jag parked on double yellow lines. They cleared the cash drawers and the safe and picked up an incoming Securicor delivery as a bonus. The second was a nighttime break-in at the home of a Hatton Garden jeweller. They tied him up together with his wife and then obtained the keys to the safe by threatening to blow the head off the wife's Pekinese dog. All in all, after expenses, they netted over a quarter of a million pounds.

Arnie had used the money—and the reputation his successes had brought him—to expand his activities and gain that precious foothold in the exclusive world of the West End.

Inevitably there'd been some aggro. A certain amount of property had been smashed, and a good friend of Arnie's called Dave Simons who had, in fact, been the third member of the successful robbery trio had been badly cut up one night after leaving Veeraswamy's Indian Restaurant down Regent Street and died in hospital the following day.

But things had settled down. Arnie's fellow villains were nothing if not pragmatists. Since they'd failed to beat him, he was tacitly accepted as having joined them. For the seven or eight years since those early, uncertain days things had gone well, business had steadily grown and problems been few and far between. The police, kept sweet by the usual regular donations, had shown no undue interest.

So it was all the more cause for concern that somebody had chucked a Molotov cocktail down the back stairs of the City Strip at half past one that lunchtime.

By midnight the club had filled with men in suits and ties and accompanied by expensively dressed women. The few unaccompanied men were catered to by the hostesses at the bar.

Arnie Bish, Phil Cavanaugh and Ginger Morrisey were still at their table. They had had food brought in from the French restaurant next door. The topic of the firebombing had been shelved but not forgotten.

"Have we any ideas?" asked Arnie. "I mean who was this bomb-happy bloody maniac? And what was he trying to tell us?"

"Not a clue," said Cavanaugh, and burped quietly.

"Ginger . . . ?" asked Arnie.

Put a gorilla in a suit and you could call it a minder; the man to be valued was the one who could not only handle himself when needed but could also assess the nature of a potential threat and distinguish between the trouble that mattered and the trouble that didn't.

Ginger shook his head. "I don't get it. Can't see who'd be benefiting."

"Business or personal?" asked Arnie. It was a question addressed to himself as much as to them, and he didn't wait for a reply but went on, "If it's somebody trying to cut our revenue then they're not very bright. They could have hit the videos, hit us nearly anywhere and hurt us worse. So is it the property they're after?"

"Wouldn't burn it down if they're after having it," offered Cavanaugh.

Arnie continued without acknowledging Cavanaugh's contribution. "I mean whose toes have we stepped on lately? Or is it somebody trying us out? Testing the defences before they come at us mob-handed?"

"What about the girl?" asked Cavanaugh.

"What about her?"

"I mean—could have been her he was after. I mean she was lucky. If the bottle had got right on the stage before bursting then she could have bought it and no mistake."

"So what about this girl then?" asked Arnie turning to Ginger.

But he was already shaking his head. "She's just a scrubber. Indian bird she is."

"So?"

"No, but I mean she hasn't got no connections or anything. I can't see it being that, I can't honest."

"And if somebody did want to make a mess of her," added Cavanaugh in agreement, "then that'd be a funny way of going about it."

There was a silence as they mulled over the mystery. Cavanaugh picked at the fragments of lobster between his teeth.

"What about . . ." said Arnie slowly, "what about that loony we had come round wanting us to have a couple of his girls in here? Phil, you were telling me about him."

"Oh yeah," said Cavanaugh. "Croxley his name was."

"You said he seemed aggrieved when you marked his card for him?"

"Oh, he did! I told him to bugger off and I thought he was going to come at me. A real nutter."

"Nutty enough to start throwing petrol bombs about?"

A more astute man might have admitted the possibility and thus avoided much of what was to follow. Cavanaugh, feeling his own reputation obscurely threatened, dismissed the idea out of hand.

"Not his style. He's just a small operator, one-man outfit. No, he's the last person I'd put it down to."

Cavanaugh had that day backed three horses to win. Two had finished way down the field and the third had to be shot after breaking a leg.

"Well, let's wait and see then, shall we," said Arnie. "Perhaps it was just some punter who didn't like the acts. But just in case it wasn't . . ." The other two leant forward to show that they were listening carefully. "In case it wasn't then I want to know of anything—and I mean any last bleeding thing—that happens anywhere. Anything that adds up to a bit of aggro or a bit out of the ordinary. Know what I mean?"

They nodded.

"I mean last thing we want is a war. I mean just in case this is some firm trying to tell us something then let's find out what it is then we can get it sorted."

"Like Churchill said," said Cavanaugh.

"What?"

"Better . . . you know, better talking than fighting . . . something like that."

"Did he," said Arnie, unimpressed. "Well, he was right, yeah. Only I'll tell you something else he said. Something that not many people know about."

"What?"

"He said—if there is going to be a war—then let's make sure we fucking well win it."

IV

It was going to be another hot day. Even as Martyn took his early morning run by the lakeside, the sun was beginning to make its heat felt. The grasses and ferns through which he jogged were tipped with brown and the pine needles underfoot crackled at his every step.

It was a run of about two-and-a-half miles that ended back at the ancient and broken-down caravan that was his temporary home but whose own siting in a field above the lake was permanent enough: its wheels had long since disappeared and been replaced by bricks. When Joe Hutton offered it to Martyn as a perk of the boat-minding job, it'd been unoccupied for two years so that Martyn had first to clean the mouse droppings from the floor and the bird droppings from the windows. The other drawbacks that Joe Hutton had thought too trivial to mention were that there was a half-mile slog to the nearest water tap and the gas mantles didn't work.

Still, it was summer and he was used to roughing it. After three years as a cosseted undergraduate at Sussex University, he'd adjusted surprisingly well to the life of an unemployed vagrant.

Back from his run, he had a strip wash in a panful of water—he'd become as miserly in his habits as any drought-stricken Indian villager—and made himself a breakfast of egg and bacon in a small battered frying pan. While it was cooking, he threw into a canvas hold-all the few essentials for his long day ahead: a packet of tuna fish sandwiches, bought in town the night before, a packet of nuts, a paperback copy of Steinbeck's *The Grapes of Wrath,* and his Sony Walkman, which was probably worth more than the caravan and all the rest of his possessions combined.

There was something else to go in on this particular morning, something that was a tight fit and threatened to squash the tuna fish sandwiches.

The caravan door didn't exactly lock—it was more a matter of jamming it—and he set out again, jogging down to the lake shore. There were now more people about, walking their dogs and savouring the air. Some were locals, with whom Martyn exchanged greetings. He was readily recognised as "the young man minding Joe Hutton's boats."

He went through his morning routine of heaving the rowing boats over onto their keels, then settled down with his back against his usual tree, took out his book and started to read. There were as yet no customers to interrupt him; the only distraction was the shimmering beauty of the lake itself which still managed to surprise him afresh every day, offering some compensation for the pittance with which Joe Hutton grudgingly rewarded his conscientious attendance.

"Anybody been to give you a medal yet?"

He recognised the voice but had to squint up against the light to see the face that went with it. It was Julie, the lady with the hip flask from yesterday. She was wearing a beige-coloured safari outfit and had her hair drawn back into a ponytail.

"No, not yet," he laughed. He uncrossed his legs, about to stand, but she dropped down beside him onto a convenient rock.

"Well, they should. I'd give you one myself only I'm fresh out of medals at the moment."

"I've got your rug," he said, pulling it from his hold-all. "And thanks very much. I hope I haven't got it dirty or anything."

"I probably saved your life," she said, taking it from him and dropping it beside her, indifferent as to whether he'd got it dirty or not.

"Probably did," he said with a smile.

There was a moment of uncertainty between them, which she covered by taking out a packet of cigarettes and lighting one. Able now to observe her without the distracting drama of yesterday, he saw that she really was a beauty. Her ash blond hair, wide green eyes and delicate features would have been stunning enough without the artfully applied makeup that highlighted them. Her hands, trembling slightly as she handled her cigarette, were tipped by nails that were finely manicured and blood red.

Out of your class. Martyn made the instinctive assessment. It wasn't just that she was older or richer. This was a lady who had altogether too much going for her to be more than temporarily diverted by the company of a beach bum squatting in a grotty caravan.

"What's the book?" she asked.

He showed her.

"Oh," she said with a shrug. It meant that she'd never heard of it and had no intention of pretending she had.

"It's about the Great Depression in America," he said helpfully.

"The Great Depression, eh? And how did they cure that? Giant doses of Valium?"

Somebody came to hire a boat, and he was busy taking their money and getting them launched. Then, as usually happened, the sight of one person taking to the water attracted more. It surprised him that when he had dealt with them all she was still there by the tree waiting for him to return.

"The man that launched a thousand ships."

"It sometimes feels like it."

"And what're you going to do when your seafaring days are over?"

"Oh . . . dunno. Start job hunting again I suppose."

"What sort of job?"

"Well, I think I've had enough of theatre management for a while. I suppose I'll just have to wait and see what comes along." He realised he was talking about himself again and so added quickly, "What about you? Do you have a job?"

"I'm retired."

"Retired . . . ?" he echoed in surprise.

"I used to be a model. In London. From which I've now retired."

"And so have you moved up here permanently or just for a holiday?"

"I'm not sure." She looked suddenly wistful. He wondered if, for all her poise and grooming, she was as uncertain about the future as he was. "I've been up here for, what, four or five weeks." Then a dismissive laugh. "Though it seems longer."

She picked up the car rug and got to her feet. He stood up beside her, sorry he was about to lose her company but seeing no way he could keep it.

"I'll see you around," he said.

She was about to return his farewell—had even partly turned away—but hesitated and, on impulse, said quickly, "Tell you what. Since nobody's given you a medal—let me buy you a meal."

He gazed at her in surprise.

"No?"

"Well, are you sure? I mean it's very kind of you . . ."

"I'm sure I'm tired of my own company. But, don't worry, I won't be mortally offended if you've got prior engagements and all that."

"No, I'd love to," said Martyn quickly. He could have kicked himself that he'd come close to offending her by his stammering response. "I would really."

"Good," she said lightly. "So. What time do you go ashore?"

He explained how it depended on what boats had been hired for what length of time, and they settled on meeting at eight in the lounge bar of the Dog and Partridge, a pub in the centre of town. After which she really did seem in a hurry to be off, striding away to her car. It was parked closer this time and he could see it was a Porsche 928S, a high-performance sports job with all the trimmings. Definitely out of his class.

Still, he was glad he'd be seeing her again and had believed her when she said that it was company she was after. Perhaps they would become friends if nothing else.

He reached for his book, then became aware he was being watched. Ten yards or so away, a trio of what he at first took to be customers were standing looking in his direction. Then he recognised one of them: a girl in blue jeans, with bare feet and a halter top. The other two, both men whom he didn't recognise, were more strikingly attired. They were bikers, in leather jackets weighted with badges and studs, well-worn jeans and thick-soled leather boots. One had hair down to his shoulders; the other a beard and mirrored sunglasses that hid his eyes.

"Hi," said the girl. "How're you?"

Her name was Wendy Harriman. She had been one of the actresses in the doomed theatre company. She was earnest and youthful and had been bitterly disappointed by its failure.

"Wendy. Hi," he responded.

"You're still here then."

"Just about. Are you still up at the hotel?"

"Yeah."

Like him, she'd stayed on to take a job in the area—waitress at the Lake View Hotel, the town's biggest. Indeed, Martyn couldn't help suspecting that it was because of him she'd stayed. In those early, heady days of May, when the company was still together, he and Wendy had enjoyed a brief sexual liaison that had ended when, sensing her growing dependence upon him, he'd gently disengaged himself from it. She had, he felt, neither forgiven him nor given up hope they might try again.

Her stance now, thumbs hooked into the pockets of her jeans and looking down at him, contained the suggestion of reproach. He realised with dismay she must have seen Julie with him. Or at least glimpsed her hurrying away to her car.

"You must come up for a drink sometime," she said. It was near to being an accusation.

"Yes," he said, a touch too eagerly, "I will. I promise."

She gave a small, knowing smile and moved away along the pebbled beach. Her two companions stared hard at Martyn, then slouched off after her. A short way along they had caught her up and were listening intently to something she was saying.

About me, thought Martyn regretfully. It wasn't so much the rotten character reference she was doubtless giving him—he could hardly complain about that. It was the realisation of how much resentment she still harboured. She clearly hadn't forgiven him for the way he'd rejected her offer of love. Perhaps all the more so because she hadn't been able to tear herself away and accept that their affair was over for good.

Julie was in the lounge bar of the Dog and Partridge as arranged and looking luscious in an ice-blue cotton suit. Martyn, who'd struggled to find a halfway decent shirt to go with the marginally better of his two pairs of jeans and had then used a whole panful of precious water in cleaning his trainers, felt obliged to begin with an apology.

"Sorry I'm such a mess. It's just that I haven't got many clothes with me."

"Neither have I," she said. "Now, what do you want to drink?"

"Oh, a half of lager please."

"And another scotch and soda," she instructed the barman.

It was a moment—when they were together and free to talk—he'd looked forward to with a growing curiosity as the day had gone on. Like most days of that summer, the sun had blazed down throughout the afternoon, and he'd been kept busy hiring boats to people seeking the relative coolness of the open water. Then, as the evening stillness had descended and the lakeside emptied, he'd been left idle, and free to consider the strange nature of his dinner date.

Was she married? He certainly couldn't remember her wearing a ring. Was she here alone? It was an odd prospect for someone whose life seemed very much in her own hands. He was intrigued.

"So," she said, when they had their drinks, "tell me all about philosophy."

He gave a little laugh. "You can't really want to know."

"Why?" she said. "Do you think I'm too stupid?"

Her directness startled him.

"It's just that most people find it a fairly boring subject."

"Try me."

He had no choice—being the guest and therefore obliged to sing for his supper—but resolved to make it short and sweet and not rattle on all night about theories of perception and Ryle's concept of mind.

"It's about the nature of reality. How we perceive it and understand it. And the way that language in particular determines the nature of that reality."

"You were right," she said.

"Pardon?"

"It is a boring subject."

He gave an unconvincing laugh and shut up abruptly, unsure whether he was being teased or insulted. Though perhaps it was neither: simply that here was a woman whose beauty had accustomed her to getting her own way and having people around her who'd pay attention to her moods and whims without her having to give a damn about theirs.

"Where would you like us to eat?" she asked.

"Anywhere," he said, suddenly wary of expressing an opinion.

"Well then how about that big hotel at the top of the town—Lake View is it called?"

"Ah well," said Martyn, alarmed. "I'd rather not go there actually. If it's all the same to you."

"Why ever not?"

"It's, er . . . personal."

A confession she found infinitely more entertaining than she had his earlier excursion into philosophy.

"Sounds fascinating. Do tell."

"I'd rather not," he said, feeling he had to make a stand somewhere.

"Then we're definitely going."

He looked at her for a hint of a smile, suspecting he was being mercilessly teased. But she gave away nothing, tapping her cigarette on the edge of the ashtray and meeting his gaze with no apparent concern for his discomfort.

"It's someone I'd rather not meet," he said, and forced himself to smile. If they were going to be sparring partners then he mustn't let her provoke him into surliness.

"Male or female?"

"Female."

"Really?"

"Yes."

He couldn't understand why she should sound surprised. Surely her arch tone had suggested all along that she'd all too readily understood his reluctance to go to Lake View.

"You seem surprised," he said.

"I am a bit, yes." And, for the first time since they'd met that evening, her face widened into a smile, gleeful and mischievous. She chuckled, as if nursing a secret joke.

"Why?" he couldn't help asking.

Then wished he hadn't.

"Because I thought you were gay. I've been certain you were gay ever since I first set eyes on you."

They went to eat in the Rockingham, a sort of bistro which she seemed to know and which Martyn would have normally considered prohibitively expensive. He hadn't really minded her thinking him gay—apparently she genuinely had—this part hadn't been teasing. But he wanted to know what it was that had made her think it.

"Oh, nothing in particular. I mean you haven't got limp wrists or anything like that. Just an impression I got, that's all. I mean the clean-cut, tall, muscular thing . . . well, it's not the sort of image that many straights go in for nowadays, is it."

Isn't it, thought Martyn. He felt suddenly provincial, out of touch with the metropolitan scene in which sexual mores were as much subject to fashion and change as were haircuts and trouser widths.

"Well, I'm not gay," he repeated. "Sorry if you're disappointed."

"It's all right," she said. "Hardly your fault is it."

So that again he found himself wrong-footed. She should have been apologising to him while he generously insisted he didn't mind in the slightest. Instead of which, he had been put obscurely in the wrong for making her think he was gay when he wasn't.

She had a magician's touch, changing everything around her, which was infuriating. It was also irresistible.

They had seafood and salad and a bottle of French white wine which she not only chose but largely drank. Without asking his permission, she smoked between courses.

Towards the end of the meal, feeling more confident and already half in love with her, he tried to uncover answers to some of his earlier musings.

"Is it a house that you have here?"

"Yes, it is." She waved a hand, suggesting out-there-somewhere. "It's in the wood. Or the forest or whatever you call it. The jungle."

"Are you there by yourself?"

Her look warned him that this was going to be no straight answer but that they were back to the thrust and parry.

"Why? Are you thinking of burgling me or raping me?" He started to smile but she hadn't finished yet. "Or you think you might end up seducing me before the evening's out? I mean now that we know you're not gay."

He was becoming used to her style and laughed. "It was an innocent question," he insisted. "But OK if you don't want to answer it."

"I live alone," she said.

They talked about the Lake District, tourists, Tarot cards and holidays which each of them had had at home and abroad. On these and a dozen other subjects she showed an evenhanded interest and chatted lightly. It was only when he tried to find out about herself that her tart replies warned him to keep his distance.

She drank two glasses of anisette with her coffee. He had a cognac and felt his head beginning to swim. The bill arrived without his ever noticing that she'd asked for it. He knew better by now than to offer to pay or share the cost. He hadn't got the money and, knowing he hadn't, she would have given short shrift to any such silly, macho gestures.

So he sat and watched as she pulled a thick wad of notes from her pocket and peeled off four or five—were they tenners?—God knew how much she must be carrying—and then said, "Right. I'll give you a lift home, shall I?"

A full moon showed him his path across the field to where the caravan stood, half hidden by nettles. Around him the silhouettes of the hills and mountains provided an epic backcloth against which he felt half pissed and fairly inadequate.

She'd driven him as far as the road allowed, then offered her hand and said a firm goodnight.

He was pleased now he hadn't spoiled things by making a last-minute, embarrassing play for her, though he might well have done had he seen any chance of success. Perhaps she knew the power of her own beauty better than he'd imagined and had kept him at arm's length so as to spare both of them the sour note on which the evening might otherwise have ended.

He recited aloud, "She walks in beauty, like the night. Of cloudless climes and starry skies . . ." It was Byron, a residue of his A-level English studies. But he couldn't remember any more and found himself yawning.

As he approached the caravan, he thought for a moment what he saw was a trick of the moonlight. So that the broken reflections in its windows didn't trouble him until he came closer.

"Oh Christ," he said. "Oh no."

It wasn't just the reflections that were broken but the windows themselves that'd been shattered, leaving only jagged shards of glass hanging in the frames.

He swore bitterly and kicked the door open. What he saw sobered him immediately. The floor and the table and his narrow bed were all littered with fragments of glass and the fist-sized rocks that had come hurtling through it.

V

The board had been full of cards. "French Model," "Black Mistress," "Young. Attractive Ex-Nurse," "Glamour Puss" . . . and two dozen more, each seeking to outdo the other in its promise of sexual bliss.

Terry had felt self-conscious, standing there in the street reading them. It wasn't the kind of thing he'd have dared do in his native Glasgow but here no one seemed to pay any attention. Other men came and went beside him, staring at the boards and even openly taking down telephone numbers. Terry, though, wasn't bold enough for that. He first read all the cards carefully, wondering on what principle he should make his choice. Then decided on the one that had "Two minutes walk from here" typed in the bottom right-hand corner. He read its phone number carefully, saying it to himself several times before he was confident he could carry it away in his head.

Still reciting it, he went to find a telephone. The underground station, he thought, would be his best bet and, sure enough, he found there a line of them separated by their acoustic hoods.

The idea that someone could easily overhear made him hesitate, but then, encouraged again by the thought that this wasn't Glasgow and frightened he might forget the number if he delayed, he went to the phone at the end of the line, checked it was working, and dialled.

"Yes?"

He'd already decided what he'd say.

"I saw your card."

"And where was that, love?"

Not expecting this, he was thrown into a small panic. He knew none of the names of the streets, certainly not the one in which he'd found the board.

"I dunno . . . I mean it was on like a board . . ."

"Oh, never mind. I'm young, brunette, thirty-eight, twenty-four, thirty-six, and it's ten pounds for hand relief, fifteen for oral and twenty for full sex."

Did he have to choose now?

"Er, yes," he said. "Yes. OK."

"Do you know where I am?"

"No," he said, not even sure where he was himself. He fumbled for something to write on, but it was too late: she was already reciting some address or other that he'd never remember.

"Sorry," he gasped. "Could you say it again?"

She did, even spelling out the name of the street—D'Arblay—so that he could scratch it down in clumsy capitals using a match on the back of his cigarette packet.

The miracle was that he ever found it. "Off Wardour Street," she'd said, so he first got himself to Wardour Street by asking people for directions and then walked up the one side and down the other before he spotted the sign that said "D'Arblay Street." It was a strange foreign-sounding name but all the more promising for that.

He'd managed to remember the number of the house, too. There was another card, handwritten this time, tacked up outside the open door, MODEL. MIRANDA. SECOND FLOOR. He stepped cautiously inside and started up the narrow staircase.

Even as he did so, there was a part of him that wished for something to happen that would prevent him from reaching the top. Or that he might get there to find Miranda already occupied. Though he knew, too, that he'd only wait if she was. Or go and find another tart somewhere else. It was a kind of insanity, this longing that overwhelmed all else.

He came to the door at the top and rang the bell. An eye looked at him through a spy-hole, the door opened and then there she was in front of him. Not bad-looking really. And young—there was no denying that. Though, had she been aged and haglike, he would probably still have gone through with it.

"I, er . . . I rang . . . gave you a ring . . ." he stuttered.

She smiled. "Come in, love."

Inside was tatty but homely. There were none of the overhead mirrors and whips for which his reading of the Sunday papers had prepared him. A few pages cut from girlie magazines and Sellotaped onto one wall were the only concessions to erotica; otherwise it reminded him of the flat he and his wife had had in Glasgow when they'd first married and before they'd saved enough to put a deposit on the house down Langley Road.

"It's ten pounds for hand relief, fifteen for oral and twenty if you want sex."

He supposed that that was what he did want.

"Twenty, yeah."

"Though for an extra five we could take our time."

"Oh . . . yes, right."

"Twenty-five then?"

He nodded. He knew he was being conned and was frightened she'd now find a way of upping it to thirty and he'd agree to that as well. Twenty-five was already twice the total of what he'd spent on presents for his wife and their baby.

"Would you like to pay me now then? Then it's, you know, out of the way."

"Yes, sorry . . ."

He fumbled for his wallet and, counting out five new fivers, noticed at the same time how little that left him for the journey back.

"Shan't be a minute, love. Why don't you be taking your clothes off, eh?"

And she patted the bed with her hand, then, taking his precious money, went off into the next room.

He started to undress, catching sight of himself in the dressing table mirror. Did any of the other lads get up to this kind of thing, he wondered. The other lads were the ones he'd met on the course, who'd come from fire services all over the country and were now on their separate ways home after last night's boozy farewell. Did they do it? Probably not, since the only time they'd mentioned tarts had been in jokes.

"Well, you are a slow coach aren't you!"

She'd come back in.

"Yeah." He gave her a sickly grin, then hurried to complete his undressing, watching at the same time as she slid off her nylon dressing gown to reveal the red underwear beneath.

"You want to help me with my bra?"

He went forward obediently and undid the clasp at the back.

"Isn't it terrible, this weather? How long do you think it's going to go on for?"

"Don't know."

"Well, I say terrible—I mean some people like it, don't they? I suppose it all depends on whether you've got to work or not. I mean it's not much fun being stuck in here all day when it's this hot."

"No."

He wondered how she could talk about her job in that down-to-earth fashion: did she not see herself for what she was?

"Still, it looks as though it might break soon, doesn't it. They were talking about storms on the weather forecast." Then suddenly, "You're Scottish, aren't you?"

"Yes."

"I like a Scotch accent. Mind you, I don't like those really thick ones that you can't understand. Well, I mean you can probably understand 'em but I can't."

She prattled on—unstoppably it seemed—as, with both of them now naked, she led him to the bed and made him lie on top of the pink counterpane. Sitting on it beside him, she asked whether he was interested in football and then, when he said he was, whether he supported Rangers or Celtic. He told her Celtic. While all the time she massaged him with a practised and indifferent hand.

"Everybody in Scotland supports either Rangers or Celtic, don't they. Well, the men do I mean. I don't suppose all the women do. But all the men seem to support one or the other."

He could have told her it was a choice made for you early on, depending simply on which school you went to: the state school, where they bred Rangers supporters, or the Roman Catholic one, where you were taught to be pro-Celtic. He himself had gone to The Holy Name of Mary down Greenlands Road. He'd been an altar boy then, serving at Mass. A few years older and he'd started going to the parish boys' club, where he'd been a promising boxer but not promising enough for it to lead to anything. Then he'd had to marry Marie when she turned out to be pregnant, and now here he was lying on a bed while a tart heaved herself on top of him.

Even before his release came, the spell that had drawn him

there seemed to have exhausted itself. He stared up at the ceiling, feeling the woman's wispy hair against his face, unable to understand how only minutes ago it had all seemed so urgent and compelling.

"You'll have a long enough journey home then," she said, climbing off him.

He nodded and swung his feet to the floor. She'd already scooped up her few flimsy garments and was disappearing into the next room.

He heard the sound of running water.

Twenty-five quid, he thought bitterly. And for what? For this speedy farce that would all have to come out in confession.

He pulled on his clothes, avoiding the mirror. She came back in, now wearing her dressing gown, and moved about the room, putting it to rights, smoothing down the bedding as though he'd already gone. In fact, clearly wanting him gone, no longer bothering with her stupid chatter about the weather and which football team he supported.

He felt himself falling under another spell, as all-powerful as the one that had drawn him there in the first place. He knew what was liable to happen next: it had happened before with Marie. He was approaching a fail-safe point; it would take only the wrong word or look from her to release all his fury and bitterness.

He tied his shoelaces, stood up and put on his tie, then his jacket.

"You got a train to catch then?"

"Yes."

"Well, call and see me next time you're in town."

His face must have betrayed his self-disgust and his determination that he never would see her again for she took a quick step backwards and restarted the bright chat.

"I don't suppose it'll be much fun travelling this weather, will it? And with so many trains now you can't even open the windows. I mean they're supposed to be air conditioned but it never seems to work . . ."

It was the smell of fear coming from her that triggered him. He swung hard at her open mouth and caught her high on the cheekbone. She gave a scream of fear, then he swung with his other hand but this time she swayed away and he missed.

She began to yell—a steady stream of obscenities—so that it was to silence her as much as anything that he grabbed her with both hands round her throat and jerked her back till her head cracked on the wall behind her.

"You rotten bitch!" he sobbed. "You rotten cow!"

He had the satisfaction—a greater one than she'd given him earlier—of seeing the terror in her face. He realised he was strangling her, dropped his hands, then hit her twice in the body and lifted his knee so that it caught her in the face as she doubled over.

She fell to the floor, scrambling at his shoes but he kicked her off and stepped back. She stayed where she was, grunting and gasping, and he saw the blood begin to well from her broken nose.

"Stupid bitch," he muttered, blaming her for all of it, for making him do it.

He thought of the money in the other room but there wasn't time to go and search. Someone might have heard the commotion. Another punter might at any moment turn up outside the door, effectively blocking his only way of escape. He had to go now while he had the chance. Sod the money.

Miranda raised her face to look at him.

"Please," she said.

The word bubbled through the blood that now covered her mouth.

"Slut," said Terry, inclined for a moment to have another go at her but wary of the blood that would mark him. "Filthy bitch."

He went to the door, listened for a moment, then let himself out, closing it behind him. Running down the stairs, he prayed there'd be no one coming up. His prayer was answered. He reached the street and set off at a brisk walk without the slightest idea where he was heading.

At length he came to a tube station and, by studying the map in the back of his diary, he was able to catch a train that took him to Euston. He collected his bag from a left-luggage locker and joined the queue for the Glasgow train. Hearing the Scottish accents around him helped him to believe he was already halfway home and to forget what he was leaving behind.

The little money he had left would allow him to eat or drink, but not both. He chose to drink and downed his first two cans of Double Diamond before the train reached Watford.

Another couple of cans and, what with one thing and another, he fell into a deep sleep. When he opened his eyes again, the train was in open countryside with what looked like a range of mountains over to the west. There were now heavy clouds in the sky, and he caught what he thought was the rumble of distant thunder.

"Where the hell are we?" he demanded.

He was told they'd left Lancaster and were on their way to Penrith. He thought back over the journey down and realised that the mountains were the Lake District. To know where he was satisfied him: he had no curiosity to think back over anything and so closed his eyes and slid back into sleep.

VI

It was the first day for weeks that the population of the lake shore —the fishermen, the families, the sunbathers—had left so early. Even before the afternoon was over, it was obvious to Martyn he was wasting his time there. He hauled the rowing boats into a line where they were out of reach of the water and turned them over onto their gunwales.

For once it seemed a necessary precaution against the possibility of rainfall: the sky was overcast and the heat unpleasantly oppressive. A thin breeze riffled the surface of the lake.

Martyn left the boats and walked up into town. He was in urgent need of some heavy duty polythene and a roll of Sellotape and, while he was about it, he'd pick up some more regular items of shopping: toothpaste, bread, soap powder and chewing gum.

This time he saw Julie before she saw him. They were both in the town's largest food store, the nearest thing it boasted to a supermarket. She was carrying a wire basket and going down the aisle parallel to the one he was in.

"Hi," he called to her across the rows of cans.

She looked up and, seeing him, gave a smile of recognition. "Well. Look who it is."

It seemed as good as an invitation to join her in her aisle, among the cereals and biscuits. He went round, wondering whether he should kiss her cheek or shake her hand and was relieved when she took the initiative, raising her face towards him and offering her pursed lips.

"You look as though you're better at this than I am," she said, surveying the contents of his basket. He looked into hers and saw she had only eggs in it—about three dozen of them as far as he could judge.

They continued round the shelves, staying together by mutual consent. She went through the checkout before him, then waited until he had paid for his shopping so that they went out together.

"Would you like a coffee?" he asked.

There was a café across the road with four tables on the pavement. It was also a shop for souvenirs, maps and guidebooks.

"OK," she said with a shrug. "Only it's your turn to pay this time."

He ordered a pastry with his coffee since he was feeling hungry; she said no, that she'd have a cigarette instead. And they sat watching the passersby while they waited to be served and thought of things to say to one another. The easy intimacy of the previous night, achieved only after considerable time and expense, seemed to be eluding them.

There was a rumble of thunder, though as yet it seemed some distance away.

"Do you think it's going to piss it down?" she asked.

"Yes," he said. "Let's just hope they don't take too long with the coffee."

"Anyway, how were your boats today?"

"All right," he said, more able now to sense when she wasn't really interested in his answers to her questions. "Oh, and listen, thanks again for the meal last night. It was very kind of you."

"Did you sleep all right after it?"

"Yes," he said in surprise.

"I didn't. I was sick. Puked it all up again."

"Oh no . . . !"

"Yes."

So she too had found an odd and disconcerting end to their evening together.

The coffee and Martyn's pastry came at last, and Julie lit a second cigarette. There was another roll of thunder, nearer this time, and people passing began to walk a little faster. There was now no one but them sitting out at the tables.

"What time did you get up today?" he asked.

"Oh, quite early. Early in the afternoon, that is."

He laughed. "I don't know how you can do it."

"I like sleep," she said simply. "It's one of the few things I'm good at."

There was a shared sense of daring in their choosing to remain out on the pavement while all around them people were glancing apprehensively skywards before hurrying off to home or hotel.

"I suppose you'll want a lift home," she said finally.

"Not particularly. It's only ten minutes."

"Oh, come on," she said, getting to her feet. "You can carry the eggs."

And they went down the now almost deserted high street, she walking slightly ahead and he following with a loaded carrier bag in each hand, to where the Porsche was parked. She opened the boot for the shopping, then they installed themselves in the low-slung seats and were on their way. She drove purposefully and without speaking.

She stopped by the field as she had done the night before but this time she got out with him as he extracted his shopping from the boot.

"Is that it?" she said, squinting into the distance. "I mean I know you said it wasn't luxurious but . . . well."

"That's it," he admitted.

They were talking about the caravan, now, in daylight, embarrassingly visible, with its mounds of bricks instead of wheels and its shattered windows.

"The windows look broken."

"They are."

She looked at him. "For God's sake, Martyn, I know you said it was old but that's a wreck!"

He shrugged. "You get used to it. At least I have. And the windows haven't always been like that."

"What happened?"

He shook his head, meaning he didn't know. "Somebody chucked stones through them. Kids I suppose."

He didn't want to tell her about his other suspicion—which was centred around Wendy Harriman and her two bikers—since it in a way involved Julie herself. If Wendy had been upset by the sight of her talking to him on the shore and had, wittingly or otherwise, encouraged the bikers into smashing up the caravan . . .

But he had no evidence to support such a notion. Perhaps it really had been just kids who, believing the caravan to be abandoned, had seen it as a legitimate target for their stones.

The storm held off for so long it seemed possible it'd missed him altogether. The thunder grumbled spasmodically but seemed content not to come any closer. It wasn't until after nine o'clock that the first flashes of lightning appeared and the first spots of rain fell. Then there was a sudden, spectacular display of forked lightning that like its accompanying thunder seemed to be directly above the town and its surrounding fells, giving erratic illumination to both. Then, without any more ado, the rain began in earnest, heavy and drenching.

The polythene Martyn had Sellotaped over the windows lasted about ten minutes. Bombarded by the rain, it slowly peeled away until the corners were gaping holes through which the rain came pouring. The piece over one window gave up altogether and went flapping away into the darkness.

Martyn crouched in the middle of the caravan, wearing his anorak for warmth. He could only watch in dismay. His repairs might have kept out the flies and perhaps the odd light summer shower. Just his luck they should be tested on their first night by a monsoon. He sat patiently watching the water stream in and tried to see the funny side of it.

The drilling of the rain on the metal roof of the caravan so dominated all other sounds that the first time he heard his name being called he dismissed it as the product of his imagination. Till he heard it again and, with it—and more difficult to dismiss—there was a banging on the door of the caravan.

He lunged forward and opened it. Outside was a figure in a yellow oilskin and holding a torch. It took him a moment to recognise her.

"Julie!" he cried in surprise. "Come in."

"Don't be so bloody stupid," she yelled back. "You come out!"

She had come to rescue him. It seemed futile to argue and anyway impossible to leave her standing there with the rain pelting into her upturned face, so he did as she instructed, stepping out of the caravan and pulling the door to behind him.

"Come on."

She started off back down the field, pointing the torch so it illuminated the ground ahead of them. Martyn squelched along beside her, wondering where they were going. Was she taking him to the YHA? Or sticking him in a hotel for the night? (Not the

Lake View, for God's sake.) Or was she taking him home, an orphan of the storm, to be warmed at her own fireside? Impossible to ask. They both had their heads down, watching for water underfoot and ducking away from the rain. There was a blaze of lightning and an almost simultaneous crack of thunder. He wondered if they might be risking electrocution, crossing in the open like this.

The Porsche was sitting in the lane at the bottom of the field, all its lights on and its windscreen wipers flicking backwards and forwards. They struggled into the front seats and finally, mercifully, were able to slam the doors on the rain.

She pushed back the hood of the oilskin so that he saw the wet ends of her hair and the tiny rivulets of water running down her face.

"Didn't expect to see you," he gasped, wiping his own face with his hand. "But thanks. I mean I really appreciate you coming."

"You're pathetic, you know that," she said, dabbing at her own face with a handful of tissues taken from the glove compartment. "First you need whisky and rugs. Then I buy you a meal because you look undernourished. And now what . . . ?"

"You save me from a sinking caravan."

"Dead bloody right I do."

He grinned—couldn't help it—but she took no notice and started the engine. Though safe enough inside the stationary car, they were again at the mercy of the storm the moment they began to move forward. The wipers managed only snatches of visibility before the windscreen refilled with exploding drops of water. It was as though they were nudging forward into a grey, dense fog. Martyn still had no idea where they were going but now couldn't ask. Julie was crouched forward, concentrating hard. There was little to distinguish the grey wall of rain ahead of them from the lakeland slate alongside.

Suddenly the wall was no longer there and they could see. On either side were sodden trees; ahead, their lights showed a narrow road that was little more than a track. They had entered the forest, where the trees arched overhead and provided a canopy that slowed and deflected the lashing rain. The car leapt forward gratefully.

Martyn looked about him. She must be taking him home then.

Certainly they were going the wrong way for the town, or for the youth hostel that was on the northern edge of it.

The car lurched and braked, throwing him forward. At the same time they seemed to be overwhelmed with a dazzling light and the harsh din of a motorcycle.

"Bastard!" shouted Julie.

Looking back, Martyn saw the motorcycle taillights going away down the track. They must have swerved and braked to avoid him. God alone knew how anybody could ride a bike in this weather.

Distracted, Martyn didn't at first notice they'd turned off the track and were slowing. They'd emerged from the canopy of trees so that the impenetrable rain had returned. The car stopped. Julie switched off the lights and wipers and pulled the hood of her oilskin over her head.

"Come on," she ordered. And she'd gone, leaving him to follow.

The rain outside greeted him like an old adversary. Looking around, all he could see was a faintly luminous rectangle over by the other side of the car. He went towards it and it became an open door leading to a hallway full of light.

It was a bungalow, if you didn't count the spare bedroom tucked away in the roof space. She gave him a perfunctory tour, pointing out what was where. By the look of things, the lounge, which was large and had a stone fireplace, was where she spent most of her time. There was a clutter of records and tapes, paperbacks and magazines. The dining room was smaller and seemed less used—no more than somewhere to keep the drinks. The kitchen, too, though modern, had a deserted air about it.

"And that's my bedroom. And that's the bathroom," she said, indicating doors off the hallway. "There's a spare bedroom up there." Pointing to the ladder that swung down to give access to the roof space. "That's where you're sleeping. OK?"

"Yes," he said. "Anything with a roof on."

She gave him a towel to dry his hair while she went to change, returning in a white dressing gown over pink pyjamas. Then she went to make toast and coffee while he put a cassette on the tape deck—Culture Club's latest album—and mooched about, inspecting the room and its contents.

What there was was there in abundance: stacked packets of cigarettes, armfuls of glossy magazines. The video recorder had a shelfful of tapes beneath it. As far as Martyn could judge from the titles, they were mostly horror films.

They sat before the electric fire and ate the toast. She produced bottles of Haig whisky and Southern Comfort and invited him to help himself. He did so cautiously.

"Have you any pictures of yourself?" he asked her. "I mean from when you were modelling?"

"Yes."

"Can I see them?"

"No."

"But why not?" he protested.

"Because I don't want you to see them. I've told you, I've retired. I'm not a model anymore. That's finished."

It didn't seem entirely logical but he could see she wasn't teasing—she really didn't want him to see the photographs—and so he didn't pursue it.

They chatted about the house. She told him it was stuck out in the middle of nowhere, had about half an acre of garden, a garage to the side and outbuildings to the back.

"What sort of a garden is it?"

She shrugged. "Flowers. Trees. What other sort is there?"

Then, around midnight, as he stifled a yawn, she instructed him, "You go to bed. I'm going to be up for ages yet."

"Well, perhaps I'd better if you don't mind."

"Why should I mind? Oh, and don't waken me if you're going to be up at the crack of dawn tomorrow. Just help yourself to anything you can find and let yourself out. Borrow the car if you like."

He couldn't believe she was serious and gave a little laugh.

"No, I mean it," she insisted. "Keys are on the hall table. Just be sure you bring it back."

He said that, of course, he couldn't possibly, then wondered whether he might. He stood up and said goodnight. As he left the room, he heard her switching on the television set.

He'd worried about wakening on time, up there in a real bed for a change, but in fact he opened his eyes at seven as he'd done every morning that summer. What he could see of the sky was an unbroken blue; there was the sound of birdsong. Evidently then the storm was long over and the summer had taken up again from where it had left off.

The lounge still held a faint haze of cigarette smoke. He came from it into the kitchen with the thought of foraging for food. At least he could be confident of finding eggs.

But, before he could begin his search, his attention was caught by a sheet of blue vellum notepaper in the middle of the kitchen table. The writing on it was an undisciplined scrawl.

"Martyn, love," it said. "Buy enough steak for two and I'll try and cook it. Say seven o'clock? Dress strictly casual. J."

Beside it and held down by a salt cruet, was a twenty-pound note.

He was to come back then. He wondered suddenly whether it was fate or conscious plotting on Julie's part that was bringing them together. He looked again at the ill-formed handwriting and remembered the three dozen eggs in the wire basket: she wasn't much of a planner. Fate then. And, since fate had managed things nicely up to now, he'd trust it to decide whether their odd, intimate-yet-distant friendship might yet turn into something more.

VII

Chief Superintendent John Forsyth listened patiently as Bob Taggart, his squad inspector, went over the details of yesterday's only serious crime in C District: the beating up of a prostitute inside her flat on D'Arblay Street. An ambulance had been called by a man who'd refused to give his name. The prostitute had been found unconscious, with a broken nose, two broken ribs and other more superficial injuries and bruising.

"Mary Jane Edmonds," the inspector read on. "Originates from Sheffield. Worked under the name of Miranda or sometimes Cindy. Seven previous convictions, all for soliciting."

"What did she have to say for herself?" grunted Forsyth.

"Says she fell and hit her head on the side of the dressing table."

End Central police station, which shared Savile Row with the bespoke tailors and the cloth merchants.

"Who's running her?"

"Donald Maloney. That's to say, he owns the lease on the property."

"And she says it was all an accident, does she?"

"Yup."

Well, if that's what the silly cow had said then why not take her at her word? Put it down to industrial injury. One of her profession's little drawbacks, the occasional beating from a loony punter.

And yet . . . there was something about it that made Forsyth hesitate before consigning the case to oblivion.

The Metropolitan Police, with its headquarters at New Scotland Yard, was subdivided into twenty-four police districts, each one known by a letter of the alphabet. C District covered an area north of Trafalgar Square and south of Oxford Street that included the majority of Soho and might therefore claim to have more than its fair share of the action. To deal with it, near enough a thousand policemen and women operated out of three stations: Vine Street, Bow Street and West End Central. Some of them were in specialist squads, such as the Street Offences Squad or the Porn Squad. Or the Licensing Office, which was headed by Chief Superintendent Forsyth and had the job of overseeing not only the pubs and clubs of the area as its title implied, but also the activities of those individuals who ran and owned them. Thus, an important part of Forsyth's job was to take a bird's-eye view of his patch, to anticipate possible rivalries or vendettas and forestall them.

He rattled a pencil against his teeth. "Do we know anything else about that fire-bombing job yet?"

"No," said Taggart. "I get the impression nobody knows much."

"Or, if they do, they're not telling."

"Well, I've had the lads do some asking around. But there doesn't seem to be a whisper so far." Then, seeing Forsyth's frowning concentration, he ventured, "Why? Do you think there's a connection?"

Forsyth shrugged. Yes. No. Who could tell? The only thing he seemed certain about these days was that he was fifty-two years old and just three weeks ago had completed thirty years service in the force. It meant that he could now retire immediately on full pension and spend his days tending his garden and listening to the radio. With a summer like this one, the prospect was increasingly irresistible.

He wrenched his mind back to the matter in hand. He was still in charge of the cesspit and hadn't written his letter of resignation yet.

"Might be a connection," he said. "Let's suppose there is. Whose was the club that got burned?"

"Arnie Bish."

"Huh. Might be just his line, beating up tarts."

"Which would mean that Maloney was responsible for the firebomb."

"Yes."

He felt less confident than he sounded. It was because his

enthusiasm for the job was slowly dying that he was pushing himself to leave no stone unturned. He didn't want them saying he was getting slack, getting past it.

"I think I'd better have a quiet word with friend Maloney and friend Bish," he said to Taggart. "Get 'em in here, will you."

"What, today?"

"Why not. If we're right and they are playing tit for tat then the sooner the better."

And if he was wrong? Well, at least he'd have inconvenienced a couple of villains for an afternoon, which was public service of a kind.

They went on to discuss other matters before Taggart left the office. Forsyth lit his first cigarette of the morning—it seemed to get a little earlier each day—and surprised himself by finding he'd come to a definite decision. He'd retire before the year was out. No question of hanging on till he was fifty-five and got the boot anyway.

It wouldn't be before time either. It wasn't just the coppers who seemed young to him; it was the inspectors. Taggart couldn't be more than thirty-five. The district commander along the corridor, to whom Forsyth was answerable, was a full ten years his junior.

What's more, he'd done his present job well, which was why they'd left him in it for over two years—longer than average since Operation Countryman left the whole force paranoid about changing the personnel of the specialist squads about every five minutes before they could get too friendly with the villains. If he was going to retire, now would be the right time. He'd be getting out while he was still on top.

At two o'clock that afternoon the chair on the other side of Forsyth's desk was occupied by Arnie Bish, who was smartly dressed in a lightweight jacket, an open-necked sports shirt, slacks and golf shoes. He was also supporting a genial smile, seeming not to mind the summons to Forsyth's office in the slightest.

Forsyth distrusted the reason for the smile. Five years ago he'd have relished the job of tracking Bish to his own lair, would have got a kick from encroaching on enemy territory. Operation

Countryman had put a stop to all that. Now you had to wait for the villains to do you the courtesy of calling in at your character-less Metropolitan Police Office, and have a witness sitting in. The villains, of course, understood the reason for this and were much entertained by the demonstration of how little the force could trust itself.

He didn't like Bish. Didn't like his poncy clothes or his cheery smile or the fact he'd got away with more than he should have.

"I believe you had some trouble at your club the other day."

"Yes," agreed Arnie. "Some berk tried to set fire to it."

"Who?"

"Search me, Mr. Forsyth. I'd tell you if I knew—believe me—but I haven't a clue."

Forsyth, who didn't believe him for a minute, took off his steel-rimmed bifocals and passed a hand across his brow.

"Yesterday," he said, "a tart got badly beaten up. It happened in her own flat. On D'Arblay Street."

Bish's expression was one of total incomprehension, but then it would have been even had he done the job personally.

"Do you know anything about it?"

"Me? No. First I've heard of it, tell you the truth. D'Arblay Street . . . ?"

"Yes." He could see him wondering and helped him out. "Donald Maloney was the leaseholder of that particular property if that's at all relevant."

"Oh. Yeah. I thought he had somewhere along there."

Might as well play his last remaining card, thought Forsyth. After all, it hadn't been much of a hand to begin with.

"Now I've had it suggested to me that Maloney might have been involved in your club getting burned. And that therefore you in turn might have had something to do with one of his young ladies being done over."

Arnie's expression was one of wounded innocence.

"Oh, come on, Mr. Forsyth. That's a load of balls. With respect. That is the biggest load of cobblers I've heard this year."

"That's how it struck me," said Forsyth.

"Oh well, I'm glad to hear it."

"I mean nobody in his right mind'd want to create that kind of aggro, would he? Because, sooner or later, he'd be the one to suffer."

"My own philosophy exactly."

I'm not doing very well, thought Forsyth sadly. I'm losing my touch. Once upon a time I'd have retained the initiative, left him uncertain as to how much I knew, made him sweat. Look at him. The bastard's enjoying it.

"What are you going to do with the club?"

"The club? Oh, we'll be business as usual inside a week. Good as new. Well, better actually."

"Maloney did you a favour then?"

Bish shrugged. "Somebody did. But then that's what you pay the premiums for, isn't it."

"You know Donald Maloney, do you?"

"I've met him."

"You get on all right?"

Arnie shrugged. "No reason not to."

Forsyth looked at him and decided he'd gone as far as he could. Might as well let it rest there.

"Well, let's hope it stays like that, eh. In fact, it'd better stay like that. Because I won't stand for any hostilities, right?"

"Understood, Mr. Forsyth."

"The days you could have your private little wars and nobody took much notice—they're long gone. And there's no way that they're coming back!"

At least not until after I've retired, he thought wearily.

Donald Maloney, who arrived at four o'clock, was an olive-skinned man with thick black hair and a gold tooth. He perched defensively on the edge of his chair.

His solicitor, who arrived with him, was a fat man sweating inside a three-piece suit. He was called Max Zabadak and needed no introduction to Forsyth who'd come across him over the years representing a variety of villains.

"You believe in taking precautions," he observed to Maloney.

Zabadak answered for him. "My client has every right to legal representation, Chief Superintendent. And he would like it to go on record from the start that he's here of his own accord and out of a wish to be of assistance."

"We're very grateful," said Forsyth drily. "And how are you, Donald?"

Zabadak allowed his client to answer that for himself.

"Oh, not too bad, Mr. Forsyth. How're you?"

"I could do without this heat."

Maloney, who was of Maltese extraction, nodded sympathetically. Zabadak's chair creaked as he shifted around, trying to get comfortable.

"One of your tenants suffered an accident yesterday." That drew no reaction from either man. "A Miss Mary Jane Edmonds. Has been know to call herself Miranda. And Cindy. When employed in the exercising of her profession."

"My client has several properties," said Zabadak. "He can't be expected to be acquainted with the private lives of all his tenants."

Forsyth ignored this and continued to Maloney, "In the opinion of the doctor who examined her she'd been beaten up. Badly beaten up."

"I'm sorry to hear it."

"Is the young lady bringing charges against anyone, Chief Superintendent?" enquired Zabadak.

"Probably not," said Forsyth. "She's under the delusion that she sustained her injuries by falling against her dressing table."

"Anything's possible," observed Zabadak, whose own career had amply demonstrated the truth of this.

"Do you know anything about who assaulted her or why?"

"No," said Maloney.

"You're sure?"

"Yes."

"Well then, you will let me know if any information comes your way, won't you?"

"Yes. But I don't think it will."

"My client will do all he can to help," said Zabadak.

"You know a strip club called the City Strip on Frith Street?"

"Yes."

"You know who owns it?"

Donald Maloney appeared to think for a moment. "Is it Arnie Bish?"

"It is. You know that somebody tried to set fire to it?"

Maloney nodded. "I read about it in the evening paper."

"Do you know anything about it?"

"Only what I read in the evening paper."

"Excuse me, Chief Superintendent," interrupted Zabadak. "Is my client being accused of involvement in the fire?"

"No," said Forsyth. "Unless he's volunteering to make a statement." Maloney didn't volunteer, so Forsyth continued, "Do you have any idea who was responsible for that fire?"

"No."

"Were you?"

"No."

"Anyone working for you?"

"No."

Forsyth smiled. It was the smile of a man who has just proved something to himself, and it made Maloney glance questioningly at his legal adviser, who said nothing but shifted again so that the chair creaked and groaned.

Forsyth spoke slowly, spelling it out. "There's been an attempt to set fire to a club. You know nothing about it. Two days later a prostitute operating from property that you own is beaten up. And you know nothing about that either?"

"No."

"You seem to know so little about either of these incidents that if you're not careful I might start thinking there's a connection between them."

There was a silence which Zabadak broke. "Was there anything else you wanted to discuss with my client, Chief Superintendent?"

"No," said Forsyth. "He can go."

Zabadak heaved himself to his feet. Maloney gave a little bow of the head.

"Thank you, Mr. Forsyth. Have a nice day."

"And you," muttered Forsyth.

He was happier with the way his talk with Maloney had gone than he'd been with the Arnie Bish interview. Zabadak or no Zabadak, there'd been moments when he'd felt he'd worried Maloney. Perhaps he really had managed to nip a potentially explosive situation in the bud. It'd be nice to think so. To feel an old hand could still show these youngsters a trick or two.

A crowd of women surged up Brewer Street and into Old Compton Street. They spilled over into the road, stopping the traffic. They were mostly young and angry and excited. Some were chanting slogans. Others carried placards proclaiming, "Women Reclaim The Night."

As they passed each sex shop, topless bar or peep show, they banged their fists on the windows and shouted at the men who might be inside. Any man who seemed to be approaching was insulted and reviled until he turned and scurried away. Then, as the crowd of women was moving away from one particular shop, a stone was thrown, shattering the big plate-glass window. The women cheered, excited by their triumph, and now began to abuse every passing male, whatever his business.

Two such were Arnie Bish and Phil Cavanaugh. They were heading for the club but had stopped to watch the feminist mob on the rampage. More stones were thrown and another window went in.

"Look at 'em," chortled Cavanaugh. "Imagine being married to that lot."

"I think they're doing a good job," said Arnie.

Cavanaugh looked at him in surprise. "Eh?"

"So long as they don't damage any of our property. Can't be bad if they're putting out some of the opposition."

Cavanaugh laughed in agreement. Still chanting, the crowd of women turned up Greek Street and disappeared from view. A police car went past, hurrying after them.

"Come on," said Arnie. "Show's over."

They carried on to the club, which had been not long open and was almost empty. They were followed to their table by a waiter with drinks and then, ten minutes later, by Ginger Morrisey.

"Did you see the dikes?" asked Cavanaugh. "There was a great mob smashing windows in."

Morrisey nodded. "They were getting some attention from the Old Bill when I came past."

"Bloody dikes," said Cavanaugh. "Jesus."

"Talking about the Old Bill," said Arnie, "I got my fair share of attention this afternoon. Got called in for a talk with Mr. Forsyth."

"That bastard," muttered Cavanaugh.

"What about, the fire?" asked Morrisey.

"Well, yeah. And something else. He was wanting to know about some brass that'd been done over in D'Arblay Street. One of Maloney's."

"I heard about that," nodded Cavanaugh.

"What, you heard who did it?" asked Arnie quickly.

"No. Oh no. I mean I just heard that she was done over, that was all."

" 'Cause Forsyth reckons it's down to us."

There was a silence as they absorbed this.

"Why?" asked Morrisey, puzzled.

" 'Cause he thinks it was Maloney that did the club."

This time the silence was even longer and the surprise greater.

"Maloney did . . . ?"

"He's another bastard," said Cavanaugh.

Arnie spelled it out so there could be no doubt. "He thinks Maloney was behind the fire at the club. Don't ask me why. But he thinks he was. And so he thinks it was us did the brass over by way of repayment."

He was rewarded with little cries of astonishment and much head shaking.

"Of course I carefully explained to him that he was a long way up shit creek as far as the brass was concerned."

"Do you think he's right about the club though?" asked Morrisey.

"You mean do I think it was Maloney that fired it?"

"Yeah?"

Arnie shrugged and then said carefully, "Let's be honest, we haven't a clue who it was. So if Mr. Forsyth thinks it was Maloney . . . well, perhaps we should give it a little thought, that's all I'm saying."

"If it was . . ." said Morrisey.

"Yeah?"

"Then he wants sorting. Very hard and very quickly."

"I couldn't agree more," said Arnie, and then repeated what they had each of them said and heard said many times before: "You show any weakness in this game and you're finished. It's got to be a case of do for 'em first and ask questions afterwards."

They nodded in agreement with the familiar catechism but then were interrupted by the arrival at the table of a stockily built, dark-haired young man who had just hurried into the club.

"Arnie? 'Scuse me . . ."

He was out of breath and worried, a condition that commanded attention.

"Adrian. Yes, what is it?" said Arnie.

"The Pigalle . . ."

It was a drinking club with a couple of well-used flats above that Arnie owned and operated in Islington.

"What about it?"

"It's been smashed up. I've just had Reg on the phone and it's a shambles. Apparently they came in mob-handed and, well, there was nothing he could do."

They exchanged a look, then Arnie said quietly, "Fucking Maloney."

"Must be," agreed Morrisey.

"You think Forsyth talked to him as well then?" asked Cavanaugh.

"No idea," said Arnie. Now grim-faced. The small gathering had suddenly become a war cabinet, unsmiling and single-minded. "But I'd lay very heavy odds it's him that's done for us."

"Our turn then," said Morrisey.

VIII

It was while they were eating the steak that Julie said, "Why don't you move in permanently? You'll only have to keep coming back every time it rains."

He smiled and said nothing, unable to tell whether she was teasing or serious and, anyway, unsure of his own feelings on the matter.

"Why not?" she urged. "I get nervous out here all alone. I've been thinking of getting a dog."

He laughed. "You think I might do instead?"

"Well at least I won't have to take you for walks."

It was an attractive idea in many ways—he'd be near to her and keeping dry—but a mixture of politeness and caution made him hesitate. He'd been sleeping on other people's floors for the past four years now and had learned to step warily. It was amazing how often a casual squat ended in tears.

"I can't just leave the caravan," he said evasively. "I'll have to go back and see what the damage is."

"Suit yourself," she said, and left it at that.

The caravan, when he got back to it, was a depressing sight. Only one of his makeshift polythene windows was still attached at all and that hung limply below the gaping hole it was meant to cover. Despite the day of sunshine, the inside of the caravan smelt damp; the mattress when he touched it was heavy with water. It needed drying out and cleaning; though, even then, with everything back to rights, it'd still be a wreck with no windows.

He heaved the mattress and seat covers out into the fresh air and collected up the bits and pieces that'd been swept to the floor by the storm. It was then, suddenly and on impulse, that he decided to do what in his heart of hearts he'd wanted to do all along: abandon both his stupid pride and the awful, sodden caravan, go back to Julie and ask if the offer was still open.

Wasn't it adolescent after all to imagine they couldn't live in the same house without having to become lovers? (And, anyway, so what if they did? Why was he skirting round that possibility with all the timidity of a virgin choirboy?) There was one thing about Julie on which he could be certain. She wouldn't stand on ceremony or be bound by any quaint bourgeois ideas of hospitality. If she didn't want him back then she'd say so.

In the event, she did exactly that—and with all the brutal frankness on which he'd been counting.

"Get lost."

"What?" he said, taken aback.

"What do you think this is, the Sally Army? I asked you if you'd stay and you said no."

"I didn't say no . . ."

"You didn't exactly fall over yourself to accept."

"I'm sorry," he said stiffly, blushing with embarrassment. "I thought you might let me change my mind."

"Supposed to be the lady's privilege."

"Yes. I'm sorry." Then, because it seemed to be the only thing remaining: "I'll go." And he turned to leave.

"Hang about!"

She caught him and, clutching his arm, guided him back into the room.

"I'm joking. Just joking."

"It didn't sound much like a joke to me."

"So it wasn't a good joke. Now stop being such a sensitive bugger and put down that bag. What've you got in there anyway?"

Not for the first time, he didn't know when to believe her. He was uncomfortable about staying but knew another walkout would bring them close to farce.

"I'd like to stay at least till the 'van dries out," he said weakly. "That's if you don't mind."

She laughed. "Is it a mess? I bet it was full of water, wasn't it?"

The question of his returning to the caravan was never again raised between them. The following day he went back alone and tried to make it as secure as possible. Two days later he told Joe Hutton he'd moved out.

"Oh, I see," said Joe Hutton gruffly. "Well, I hope you won't expect to be paid any more on account of it. That was accommodation that went with the job you know."

"I know," said Martyn, with a disarming smile. He'd been ridiculously underpaid from the start; there was little point in making a stand now.

Joe Hutton gave a mollified grunt, then asked, "So where are you staying then?"

"At . . . at a friend's."

"Hmm. That friend with the Porsche is it?"

"Yes," said Martyn, and turned away to deal with a customer. He certainly wasn't going to be drawn into an elbow-nudging conversation in which he was leeringly congratulated over his success in moving in with Julie. That would have been a crude and unworthy betrayal.

His days now assumed a new pattern. Early each morning he descended from his loft, went for a run and returned to breakfast alone. There would be sticky glasses and piled ashtrays in the lounge, evidence of Julie's late nights. It occurred to him she must always retire to bed either drunk or as near as damn it.

After breakfast it was down to the lake shore where, as the summer continued, so did his job of boat minder. Occasionally Julie put in an afternoon appearance, joining him for a chat and a smoke, but, as often as not, he didn't see her till the evening when he returned to the bungalow. At first she cooked for them both and they ate with their plates on their knees around the television set, then she suggested a run out and it became a regular thing: they'd drive blindly for a half hour or so, then stop somewhere to eat.

"Why don't you do the driving?" she'd invited him. "Then I can concentrate on the drinking."

He'd readily agreed and thereafter always took the chauffeur's role. He also attempted to do his share of the paying but couldn't keep up with their extravagant life-style that Julie was happy enough to go on funding.

"For Christ's sake," she said one night after they'd had their customary argument over the bill, "look at this lot, will you."

And she'd pulled open the bottom of the four kitchen drawers. It contained wads of notes, new ones, still held in their bank bindings.

"Have a look," she said. "Count them if you like."

He gingerly picked up the top bundle, whose binding said "£500" and which comprised ten-pound notes. Then, not sure what he was supposed to do with it, he replaced it carefully on its pile. There must have been five or six thousand pounds altogether.

"It is real," she said drily. "Or if it isn't then the bank's been doing me."

Martyn, who'd been brought up to respect wealth and treat it with care, was scandalised to find this horde of cash lying around in the kitchen below the cutlery and the tea towels.

"You're just asking for it to be stolen."

"Who by?" she laughed. "Who in their right mind would look for money in the kitchen?"

She had a point but he still felt bound to protest.

"It's an awful lot of money."

"Exactly. So you can stop feeling that your macho pride's been hurt every time I spend some of it." She closed the drawer. "I'd say take some but I know you'd refuse."

He would, yes. It was bad enough accepting meals from her; cash would have been impossible. For the same reason he was determined to keep his boat-minding job: so that he'd retain his independence and not feel some kind of household pet, kept on for company and instead of a watchdog.

Slowly, and with no intention of prying, he learnt new facts about her. Her second name was Eden—that came from the odd item of post that arrived; she still had a flat in London, somewhere in Clapham; she'd never been married or engaged or had children—this much she told him; she couldn't swim or ride a bike; he observed for himself that she'd no interest in sport or politics or the arts; one evening he took her out on the lake and discovered that, though she insisted on trying, she couldn't row either.

They became lovers during his third week at the bungalow. Looking back on it later, Martyn decided it was mainly because they'd both stopped being on guard against it. The danger period—his first few nights on the premises—was over. They'd established a routine that didn't include sex and so had relaxed and stopped caring about where they were sitting and whether they were touching.

With the result that they'd ended up screwing on the floor of the lounge with the television set still on behind them. They'd been for their customary evening meal, shared a bottle of wine, and then shared another one when they'd got back. She'd sat on the floor beside him, their playful embraces had become serious, and it'd happened without a word being spoken.

It was the aftermath that shocked him.

She got to her feet and said, "Right, you can go now then."

He looked at her in surprise. Was this some kind of postcoital joke?

"I said you can go. You've got what you came for—so get the hell out of here will you."

It wasn't a joke. She was bitter and angry and meant every word of it.

He scrambled to his feet. "Look," he said, "I'm sorry about what's happened if it's upset you. But it's not . . . what I came for."

"Get out. Go on."

She wouldn't look him in the eye but concentrated on the cigarette she was lighting.

"Right then, I'll go," he said simply.

He went up to his attic bedroom, flung everything that was his into his hold-all and came back down the ladder. There were, he knew, other items belonging to him here and there about the place but these he would have to forfeit. She wanted him out, and out quickly, not wandering about searching for belongings.

It was a starry night and still warm. He set off down the track without knowing where he was going. The caravan? It was a possibility. Another was to sleep under one of the upturned boats on the beach. Apart from the odd screech of a hunting owl, his own footsteps were the only sound accompanying him along the track. It would have been eerie had it not become such a familiar territory during the days he'd stayed at the bungalow. Then he heard a car start in the distance and knew she was coming after him.

He had time before she reached him to wonder what new game she was playing and how he ought to react. Should he go back? Or wasn't he after all best out of it? She was irrational and volatile. And, OK, she was lovely and he'd never have left of his own free will. But, now she'd sent him packing, surely he should count his blessings, resist her appeals and keep on walking.

The Porsche came up behind him, its headlights throwing forward a giant silhouette of himself along the track. He stepped to one side and for a moment thought she wasn't going to stop.

It was a moment in which his own heart betrayed him by its leap of fear that she might not want him back after all.

But she'd jerked the car to a stop twenty yards down the track and swung open the passenger door. He came to it and leant down to look in at her.

"Hello."

"Get in."

"Why?"

"Why do you think?"

But he was determined to oppose her and remained where he was, leaning over the car door.

"I'm sorry," she said. "All right? I was stupid. So will you get in for Christ's sake?"

He hesitated still, but now it was a charade to save face. Then he bent down and climbed into the car, pulling his hold-all in after him.

She drove them to the bottom of the track where there was room to turn, then swung the car in a tight circle and brought them back to the bungalow. She began to laugh.

"What's funny?" he asked, frowning.

"You. Marching off with your bag. Looking all hurt and forlorn but being ever so brave about it."

Her refusal to take his feelings seriously was infectious. Despite everything, he found himself smiling so that by the time they got back indoors the rift was healed between them.

The sequel waited until he returned to the bungalow the following evening after his day by the lake. He hadn't seen Julie all day

—which wasn't unusual—and now, coming through the unkempt garden, he wondered how she'd greet him. Would their night of love remain as an awkward impediment to their friendship? Or had their reconciliation got them over and beyond that?

"Hi."

"Hi."

She kissed him.

"Come on. Something I want to show you."

She was leading him away from the door and round the side of the house.

"What?"

"There," she said, and nodded towards the patio, which generally had a few sticks of weather-beaten furniture on it but was now the stage for something quite different.

It was a motorcycle, a creation of blue and black bodywork and silver chrome. And it was a monster, gleaming and majestic, with a four-stroke engine of over a thousand cc capacity. Lettered on the side was "Suzuki" and "GS1100G."

"I said the biggest they'd got," said Julie, watching his face. "Is it all right?"

"It's fantastic," muttered Martyn, still not clear what was going on. "Do you mean you've bought it or what?"

"You said you used to have a bike."

Had he said that? If he had, he'd been referring to the old two-stroke BSA he'd bought secondhand when he was sixteen.

"I did, yes. Not one like this though."

"It's for you. It's a present."

He'd placed a tentative hand on the controls but now stepped back as though he'd received an electric shock from it.

"No . . . !"

"It's no good to me. I can't ride the thing."

"But I can't . . ." He shook his head. "You shouldn't have."

"I wanted to apologise for seducing you. And then for kicking you out afterwards."

He stepped towards her and took her in his arms, but she flinched away.

"Do you like it?" she said quickly.

He saw that she'd talk only about the bike, not about them.

"Of course I do. It's a marvellous bike but . . ."

"But nothing. Let's go for a ride, yes?"

He tried to find objections but found only that she'd arranged everything—insurance, crash helmets, the lot. He swung his leg across it and heaved it from its stand. It was a weight; handling it would be a challenge.

"We'll find somewhere to eat," said Julie, climbing on behind him. "Some run-down café with a jukebox. The sort of place where people with motorbikes always stop."

It was a game to her, a new toy. As at one stage he himself must have been and maybe still was.

The engine fired at the touch of a button. Martyn let out the clutch, allowing the bike to creep forward. It was a while since he'd ridden, and he didn't want to take any chances. They came down the track between the trees, then onto the road and were heading northeast towards Grasmere. He was beginning to get the feel of it, though he was still cautious in cornering and reluctant to use more than a fraction of the power it offered.

"Great," yelled Julie into his ear. "Can't we go faster?"

He still knew so little about this woman who was clinging to his waist. She seemed to live for kicks, yet had shut herself away, hermitlike, high above Coniston Water; she was guarded and hostile, even with him who was her lover; she was reluctant to talk about her past or give any thought to her future. And she'd bought him a motorbike.

It'd already been a summer to remember, and they were still only in the last days of August. The hot weather was holding; it almost seemed that the climate had taken a permanent turn for the better. Only the occasional chilling breeze that rose from the lake in the late evening gave a hint of what was to come.

IX

It was a quiet evening until, a little after nine, a group of skinheads entered the main bar. There were eight of them, all in tee-shirts and jeans, emblazoned from head to foot with obscenities and the letters NF. Their heads were virtually clean-shaven and, despite the weather, they were wearing boots.

They came to the bar and spread themselves along it, laughing for no obvious reason and talking loudly. The few other people in the pub fell silent and watched, until their looks were met with hostile stares and they quickly turned away. A young man and his girlfriend left their drinks and sidled out of the pub, their heads down.

"Yes, lads?"

Vincent Cudworth, who'd come forward to serve them, had no taste for heroics and could smell trouble as clearly as anybody else but, unlike them, couldn't sidle out. His name was above the door, "licensed to sell ales and spirits." A licence to kill might have helped; without it, all he had to offer was affability, the welcoming smile of the helpless. That and an old police truncheon under the bar and away to his right where the glasses were stood to drain.

"What'll it be then?"

The skinheads had stopped talking and jostling one another and were looking at him. He could hear his wife shuffling nervously behind him, not knowing whether to come to his side or go to the phone. The phone, you stupid bitch, he thought.

Then the biggest of them, who had NF painted in blue on his forehead, leaned forward over the bar and said, "Pints, landlord." At which the others laughed.

"That's, what, seven . . . eight pints then, is it?" said Vincent, beginning to pull the first one. "Pints, love," he said to his wife and she joined him so that they were both pulling furiously at the old-style pumps, desperate to give the skinheads something to distract their attention and keep them happy.

The pub was called The Little Lieutenant and was just off New Bond Street. Way off the beaten track for yobboes like these, it was in an area of upmarket shops and restaurants, jewellers, auctioneers and art galleries. It was a lunchtime pub as much as anything, doing meals and bar snacks and with little custom in the evening. Which was why Vincent had no other help just now but for his wife and a young girl.

And now this lot had breezed in, this party of boneheaded predators.

"Four," he counted, placing another pint on the bar.

The skinheads now had the pub to themselves. Everybody else had gone, the men hustling out the women as though they were concerned for their safety only and not their own. Maybe the skinheads were just up west for the night, prayed Vincent. Getting their kicks out of scaring people—nothing else. Well, they'd scared him all right. Might that not be enough?

"Seven," he said. His wife was pulling the eighth pint. "That's five pounds seventy-six."

There were one or two guffaws of laughter as they each took a pint and began to drink.

"Who's paying then?" asked Vincent. His heart fell. It wasn't going to be that easy after all. "Come on, lads, who's got the money then?" He rubbed his hands and smiled at them. The scum, the snotty-nosed, mindless apes—he hated them but he kept on smiling. Perhaps if he insisted on seeing it as a joke they'd end up going along with him.

"Nobody's paying," said the biggest of the skinheads.

"Well, somebody'll have to," said Vincent.

His wife had at last disappeared round the back of the bar. Ring anybody, thought Vincent. Ring the police, ring Maloney, ring the speaking-fucking-clock but get some help so he could get these evil, spindly creeps off his premises and back out into the night from where they'd come and where they belonged.

Most of them were drinking greedily as though in a hurry, knowing they hadn't long. The biggest skinhead, though, had taken only a sip off the top of the beer.

"I think there's something wrong with this," he said.

"All that's wrong with it is that I'm still waiting to be paid," said Vincent evenly.

The betraying tinkle of a telephone number being dialled came from behind the bar. The biggest skinhead heard it and looked at Vincent.

"Now come on," said Vincent. "Don't let's have any bother."

"Cat's piss," said the biggest skinhead and tipped up his glass so that the beer poured out over the bar top.

"All right then!" shouted Vincent. "That's enough! Outside. Come on, the lot of you, let's have you outside!"

It was a show of bravado that only emphasised his helplessness. They laughed and shouted obscenities back at him, then one of them threw a glass at the frosted mirrors that lined the walls. The glass shattered and the mirror, two hundred pounds worth of it, cracked and fractured. Vincent cursed and grabbed the truncheon.

It was also their cue for action. Other glasses were flung and, where the mirrors withstood them, one of the skinheads picked up a bar stool and lunged at them until they were all fragmented. The lights were brought down, smashing the mock-Victorian shades that'd cost over fifty pounds each.

A skinhead who had a crown of thorns tattooed around his head pulled out a flick knife and went round slitting the upholstered seating. Another followed him, cutting the backs of the seats with a razor.

An ashtray was thrown and went crashing through a window. It was a compelling example they all wanted to follow and, within seconds, every window in the place was smashed.

Watching all this, half-crouched behind the bar, Vincent became aware that they didn't seem too interested in damaging him, just the property. Unless they were saving him for some brutal finale. He gripped the truncheon and waited, grunting with fear and fury.

Then the biggest skinhead shouted, "Right, come on, get out." And, with a final yell of triumph and a last kick at the furniture, they all made for the door.

"Goodnight," said the biggest skinhead as he followed them. Seeing now that he was safe—they weren't going to do for him

—Vincent yelled, "I'll get you for this!" He was trembling and near to tears.

Their heavily shod feet went away into the distance. There was a sudden quietness that was unbelievable, just the faint sound of traffic and an aeroplane passing way above.

"Vince . . . ?"

It was his wife, crawling round on her hands and knees from where she'd taken shelter behind the bar.

"They've gone."

"Are you all right?" she said fearfully. "They haven't hurt you, have they?"

"I'm all right," he said. "Thank Christ."

She put her arms round him and held him. The police arrived five minutes later to find them still there behind the bar in one another's arms.

Arnie Bish grinned. He liked it. Phil Cavanaugh and Ginger Morrisey added their appreciative chuckles to the reception the tale was receiving.

"So it's all down to a gang of yobboes?" asked Arnie.

Adrian Donnachie nodded. "No connection with us."

"Did these yobboes know what they were doing?"

Adrian shook his head. "No. Except for the one I told you about, the big lad. The others'll do anything he tells them."

"So you think he's keeping all the money for himself?" asked Phil Cavanaugh.

"I'm sure he is."

There was another chuckle of appreciation.

"Sounds like he might be a useful sort of lad when he gets older," said Ginger.

Adrian nodded earnestly. He'd promised to put in a word. It'd been part of the deal he'd made with Jake, the big skinhead. Fifty quid and a recommendation that might—just might—lead to regular employment. All he had to do in return was round up a bunch of his compatriots and make an unholy mess of The Little Lieutenant, a poncy lunchtime boozer off New Bond Street. Which, although he didn't bother mentioning it, was owned by a Mr. Donald Maloney. In fact, it was one of Maloney's few legitimate fronts, a recent acquisition at no small expense, the apple of his eye and the last place on earth he'd want to see a load of urban redskins going berserk.

"You've done well, Adrian," said Arnie.

"Thanks."

"Only lay low a while, eh. I know you say there's no connection but there's always the possibility, you know what I mean? Go away somewhere, take a holiday."

Adrian nodded.

"Now go and have a drink. You've earned it."

It was his dismissal. He left the three of them at the table and, flushed with his success, went to the bar. It'd been his first commission, the first time he'd been expected to act on his own initiative.

"I want us to hit back at Maloney," Arnie Bish had said. "And I want it so's there'll be no comebacks from the coppers. Nothing to say it was us in other words. In fact I don't want to know about it till after it's happened. Just clear it first with Ginger here, OK?"

The responsibility had frightened him to begin with, until he'd thought of Jake who was mad enough to do anything for a few quid and the thought that he might be advancing his chances of promotion to the big league. And it'd all worked out. The pub had been left a shambles and the skinheads had made an easy getaway on the tube. He'd met Jake an hour later to hand over the money, then hurried to report to Arnie at the club, confident the evening's work would have done his own reputation no harm at all.

Arnie Bish and his two companions watched him as he went to the bar.

"Good lad that," said Phil Cavanaugh.

"Yes," said Arnie Bish abruptly. "So where do we go from here?"

It was Ginger Morrisey who answered.

"Time we started talking."

"To Maloney?"

"Yes. Least that's my advice. Otherwise he's going to try and hit us again. And then we'll have to call out Adrian's bunch of loonies again. And sooner or later it's going to get serious."

Arnie nodded slowly in agreement. "You mean it'll be bodies instead of pieces of furniture?"

"I do. And the only way to stop it is to talk. Talk to Maloney and let him know we're willing to call it a day if he is."

Arnie Bish thought for a moment, then said, "All right. You set it up then."

"When for?"

"Sooner the better. Otherwise he'll be having another go at us, and we'll be obliged to have another go back."

"Tomorrow then."

"What's wrong with tonight?"

Ginger Morrisey thought about it. "Nothing."

"He might be a bit upset about his boozer being smashed up," offered Phil Cavanaugh.

But Arnie waited for Ginger's next observation.

"He's a businessman. I shouldn't think he'll be too upset to work out how much money it might end up costing him if there's a real war starts."

"So, like I say, why don't we meet him tonight."

Ginger Morrisey nodded, got to his feet and went through to the office where there was a telephone and he could make the first approaches that would lead to a meeting with Donald Maloney. Arnie Bish and Ginger Morrisey stayed where they were and signalled for more drinks.

X

It took Martyn only a couple of days to get the feel of the bike and then he began his travels in earnest, exploring the lakes as far as Ullswater in the north and Ennerdale in the west. As much as Julie's gift, it was Joe Hutton's new and unexpectedly generous attitude that made such journeyings possible. Perhaps it was Hutton's conscience that was pricking him, or perhaps it was his wife —anyway, he'd taken to wandering down to the lake shore in the late afternoon and taking over the boat minding so that Martyn could finish early.

Julie, for her part, seemed to have exhausted her interest in pillion riding on that first trip. When Martyn asked her if she'd like to come with him on his expeditions, she answered, direct as ever, that no, she didn't. He also came to realise that she wasn't too keen on seeing him back at the bungalow before six or seven in the evening. She'd then be eager for his return and greet him affectionately enough. But she liked her days to herself.

They were into September and there were signs the sun was beginning to lose its grip, particularly in the evenings which had begun to turn chilly. It was on a day that was noticeably overcast that Joe Hutton came down at lunchtime, his earliest visit to date.

"You might as well go," he said to Martyn. "There's not going to be much happening this afternoon."

Martyn began to thank him but was stopped.

"I don't know how much longer I'll be able to keep you on, to tell you the truth. I generally reckon the season's over by the second week in September."

So he was getting the push. Hardly surprising. Boat minding must rank among the least permanent of occupations.

"I'll stay as long as you want," said Martyn with a shrug.

"Say another week then," said Joe Hutton abruptly.

Riding away up the road, Martyn found unemployment an

uncomfortable prospect. It wasn't that he bore any animosity: he'd been grateful for the job and indifferent to the meagre payment or the grottiness of the caravan that'd gone with it. It was the future that he now resented. Would he now have to leave the bungalow? Leave Julie?

He pushed the bike along, finding the roads quieter now there were fewer tourists. He was heading north towards Langdale Fells, hoping his early start would let him explore the northern lakes of Thirlmere and Derwent Water.

As he came over a steep rise and began to descend, he caught sight of a car some two or three hundred yards ahead of him that he immediately recognised as Julie's Porsche. Or someone else's Porsche, identical to it. He began to draw closer, thinking it would be fun to surprise her but, before he could get near, the Porsche had slowed and turned, leaving the main highway and disappearing down a snaking one-track road that was signposted "Stone Crags."

He couldn't have explained, even to himself, why he there and then abandoned his plans for visiting Thirlmere and Derwent Water and instead slowed and turned to follow the Porsche down the narrow road. Was it the innocent hope of surprising her, or the less worthy one that he might find something out, discover her at some secret rendezvous perhaps? Riding along the track, he told himself he must turn back, this was an unfair and mean trick and she'd be furious if she found out. But somehow, each time he promised himself he'd turn, there was another rise or twist in the road that he was curious to see beyond. So he went on, catching glimpses of the car ahead of him.

Then even they stopped. He was beginning to wonder if he'd lost her altogether when he saw the walls of what might have been a large house but for the sign by the gate: ORDER OF ST. JOHN. HOLY ROSARY HOSPITAL.

He stopped and looked in through the open gate. There was a cluster of buildings, mainly old and made of stone, though with the odd prefabricated extension, and a dusty car park in front of them. The Porsche was parked there. Julie had got out and, her back towards him, was disappearing up the front steps and into the main building.

Martyn hesitated, but knew he'd no option but to go after her and admit to having followed her. To turn round and ride off would put him in the role of spy.

He engaged the clutch and let the bike carry him through the gate and onto the car park where, beside the Porsche, there were another two cars and an old minibus. It was a hospital—the sign had said so—but there was precious little evidence of any kind of activity. The place was peaceful to the point of seeming deserted.

Martyn climbed off the bike and removed his helmet. The front door to the hospital opened again but it wasn't Julie. It was a nun. She was dressed in white, a sort of compromise between nun's habit and nurse's uniform, and wore a short white veil around her head.

She was about to cross to one of the other buildings but then, seeing Martyn, detoured towards him and called out, "Good afternoon. Can I help you?"

Martyn cleared his throat. "I'm waiting for someone, thank you." He wondered if he should address her as "Sister."

"One of our patients?"

Not sure of the correct answer, he indicated the car alongside him. "It's a Miss Eden. She's just gone in."

"Ah yes. And does she know you're here?"

"Probably not, no."

"Oh well then, I'll tell her. And you can wait inside. Would you like to come this way?"

He'd no alternative but to follow. She spoke and moved with such assurance that refusal was impossible. They went into the entrance hall and were met by a smell of antiseptic and floor polish. On one of the walls, which were painted green, a recess supported a statue of Our Lady of Perpetual Succour.

The nun left Martyn there on the bench while, despite his protestations that he was happy to wait forever if need be, she went to find Julie and tell her she had company. Martyn gave a small groan of dismay at the silly situation he'd got himself into. She was sure to be furious, thinking he'd been spying on her.

The nun returned and gave an encouraging smile.

"She won't be very long."

"Oh. Thank you."

"My name is Sister Veronica by the way. I know Miss Eden—Julie—quite well."

Martyn stood up and offered his hand. "I'm Martyn."

She responded with a brisk, dry handshake, then left him alone, apologising for the fact she had work to do. Martyn watched her go, wondering at the strangeness of the life she must lead and how she, or anyone else, could give themselves to it.

The entrance hall offered little in the way of clues to what went on inside the hospital that made it such a haven of tranquillity. There were a number of illuminated scrolls, framed and behind glass, hanging on one wall. Martyn went to read them and found they were the names of benefactors.

He'd been waiting twenty minutes and was enjoying a pleasant doze when suddenly there was Julie come from along the corridor and standing in front of him.

"I'm sorry," he said quickly, getting to his feet. "I mean about being here. It just sort of . . . well, one thing led to another."

"I was told there was a handsome young man who looked like he might be a Hell's Angel waiting for me," she said.

There was a wry half smile on her face. At least then she wasn't furious with him. Or was that still to come?

"I look like a Hell's Angel . . . ?"

"You did to Sister Veronica."

He allowed himself a laugh. Then saw that Julie was still waiting for an explanation.

"I was out on the bike," he said, "and I saw your car. And, well, I thought I'd follow you for a joke. I mean I wasn't spying on you or anything."

"You mean you weren't spying very well."

"I wasn't spying at all," he insisted.

"So I suppose you now want to know what I'm doing here?"

"Not if you don't want to tell me."

She looked at him for a moment, then said, "You managed to follow me here. Do you think you can follow me home as well?"

She refused to say anything until he'd made her a pot of tea and brought it to where she sat smoking in the lounge.

"Thank you."

"Listen, though."

"What?"

"I am sorry about following you like that."

"Oh, stop apologising. You want to know what I was doing there?"

He started to protest that he didn't, that she had every right to her privacy, but he saw the look of bored disbelief on her face and so said instead, "Yes. If you really want to tell me."

She began with the air of one who was determined to tell the whole truth, starting at the beginning.

"It's a small private hospital run by the nuns of the Order of St. John."

"Yes."

"And they're saints," she said. "They're all of them absolute saints."

Her look challenged him to deny it.

He nodded. "Yes."

"And they deal with people who're either mentally disturbed or alcoholics or drug addicts."

"I see."

"So now I suppose you're wondering which I am."

He knew better than to try and answer that, so waited until she went on. "I had a friend, a very good friend, and she was a drug addict. She was someone I knew in London and she was on heroin. And when she tried to get off it, she came up here and they looked after her."

"Did she . . . did she get off it?"

Julie gave a small shrug. "The first time, yes. Because they're marvellous. As I said, they're absolute saints."

"The first time . . . ?"

She nodded. "She stayed off for six months. But then went back on it and came up here again. Went into the hospital again. Only this time she'd brought some heroin with her. Secretly. And she took it and, what with the methadone and everything, she overdosed herself."

"She died?"

"Yes."

"I'm sorry."

"So was I." She stopped for a moment, then resumed, "Anyway I've been back there a few times since. To give them money and help in other ways."

"I see."

The explanation came as something of a relief: so she wasn't suffering from some dreadful terminal disease or going to visit someone else who was. There had been a tragedy but it was behind her and in the past.

A thought struck him. "Is that why you left London? I mean gave up the modelling and everything? Because of what had happened to your friend?"

"I suppose it was," she admitted. "It was a life that'd always had its seamy side. Drugs and the rest. For a while it was quite attractive, but then . . ." She shook her head. "If you'd seen the way this friend of mine changed. She was once very beautiful."

"Was she a model?"

"Yes. And in films. Except that, by the time she died, she hadn't worked for, oh, over a year, she'd changed that much. Poisoned herself."

"Thanks for telling me," he said gently. "And I'm still sorry for following you."

She shrugged. "I'm glad you did."

The subject was dropped until that night when they'd gone out to the Rockingham for a meal.

"Have you ever seen anyone who's having withdrawal symptoms?" asked Julie suddenly.

"No."

"It's terrible. They're sweating and vomiting, can't sleep, and they have these awful pains in their guts. I mean that can kill them. Never mind the heroin, even if they kick that then the bloody withdrawal symptoms can kill them."

The waiter brought their soup and Martyn waited for him to retreat before asking, "Don't they give them something to help them through all that though?"

She nodded. "Methadone."

"Is that a drug?"

"Yes. But it's not injected. It's a kind of linctus that they take orally."

"And does it help much?"

"It can do. Only they can't give you too much, or else you end up finding that you've come off heroin but you're hooked on methadone and so you've still got it all to come."

He grimaced. "You can't win."

"Some do," she said. "But not many."

He thought she was going to cry and reached across to take her hand. But she wouldn't let him and kept her face down, concentrating on her soup.

"Anyway," she said, "tell me about the boats. Why weren't you minding them this afternoon instead of following me about all over the place?"

He told her about Joe Hutton's new-found generosity in letting him finish early.

"Good of him," she said tartly.

"Well, yes. Except that I think it's really his way of giving me the sack."

"Really?"

"Definitely. The summer can't go on forever you know."

"So when are you . . ." She hesitated. Like him, she seemed to shy away from confronting the future. "When do you finish?"

"Next week."

She said nothing, so he added, "I thought I might go down to my parents for a couple of days."

"Near Bristol?" she said, remembering what he'd told her.

"Yes. It's their wedding anniversary."

"You'll be going down on the bike?"

"I suppose so," he said. "I hadn't really thought about it."

They ordered more drinks and finished the meal in high spirits. Neither wanted to return to the awful subject of heroin and the death it'd caused; nor did they want to look too closely at the future where uncomfortable decisions waited to be made. So they drank a lot, then went home and watched one of Julie's horror videos, a story of murder in which the victim returned to haunt his assailant. After which they went to bed, made love and fell asleep.

XI

"Has this trouble blown over do you think?"

"Yes, sir. I do, yes," said Forsyth decisively. It was all he could say. Anything else and he couldn't in all conscience tender his resignation. Only if everything had blown over was the stage set for him to leave.

"Any prosecutions?"

"No, sir."

"None?"

"In my opinion we've nothing that'd stand up in court."

"But you are sure there isn't an ongoing feud there?"

Forsyth nodded. "I've spoken to the two villains principally involved and read 'em the riot act. Of course neither would admit to anything but I got the distinct impression both were ready to call it a day."

It was his weekly reporting session with the district commander, taking place in the commander's office on the top floor of West End Central police station. It was a familiar procedure; his awareness of the letter in his pocket didn't alter that.

The commander was square of jaw and shoulder and had blond hair swept straight back. He couldn't have been more than forty-ish, which suggested promotion so rapid as to be dizzying. It was because of his youth that Forsyth had persisted in addressing him as "sir" in place of the first-name terms that most senior officers adopted in private. It was as though he had to keep the other man's seniority permanently in view.

"So what about the pub in Bond Street? The Little Lieutenant is it called?"

"Yes."

"Looked like a bomb had hit it from what I'd been told."

"There was quite a bit of damage, sir, yes. According to the manager it was a gang of skinheads . . ."

"I've read the report," said the commander, cutting him short.
"In which you suggested that it was almost certainly a put-up job.
Do you still think that?"

"Yes, sir."

"So who was behind it?"

Forsyth shrugged. "Arnie Bish. At least if I'd any money then
that's where I'd be placing it."

"You've had him in?"

"Oh yes. Like I say, I've been reading the riot act to a lot of 'em
recently. And I think you'll find that it's done the trick."

Following the mayhem in The Little Lieutenant, his threat to
Bish had been clear enough: you foul up the last days of my
career and, as sure as night follows day, I'll foul up the rest of
yours. Little more had been needed: just a hint that there were
old files lying around that could always be reopened and supplemented by Forsyth's own private information. It was, admittedly,
information that was double-edged, incriminating police officers
as well as villains. For this reason Forsyth, whose first loyalty was
to the force, had kept quiet.

Now, though, he was leaving. Knowing that made him feel less
protective towards the reputations of his fellow officers and ex-
officers. If Bish and Maloney continued their little games then
he'd do everything he could to put both of them inside, regardless of cost.

Bish, who was villain but no fool, had understood him, he was
sure of that.

"But no prosecutions," repeated the commander.

Forsyth kept calm and repeated his answer. "We've nothing
that'd stand up." What did the man want? That they should go to
court and be made fools of?

"A pity."

"Yes, sir."

Then, recognising that Forsyth wasn't going to budge, he let
the matter drop.

"Well then, and is there anything else?"

"Just this, sir." Forsyth took the envelope from his pocket and
laid it on the desk.

"And what's this?"

"My resignation."

The commander gave an "Ah!" of surprise, slit the envelope with a paper knife and took out the single sheet of paper inside.

Must be good news for him, thought Forsyth. Another of the old school out of the way. Soon this new generation of coppers'd have the force to themselves. Better educated and better armed, it was only surprising they didn't seem able to get any better results.

"I don't suppose I can persuade you otherwise," said the commander, which meant he wasn't going to try.

"I shouldn't think so, sir, no."

But, if he wasn't going to persuade him, he was at least going to do things properly and, leaving his desk, he produced a sherry bottle and two glasses from a cupboard.

"So," he said when they'd got drinks in their hands, "and what will retirement hold for you then, eh?"

"Oh, one thing and another. Nothing very spectacular."

"You're something of a gardener I gather?"

"Yes, sir. And we've had a caravan for five years that's barely had a chance to move. Planning to get some use out of that."

It sounded mundane and predictable when he said it but it was a prospect he privately treasured: to be at last climbing out of the pit, leaving the ponces and the tarts and the villains and the eternally stupid punters to stew in their own juices.

"Will you be looking for another job?"

Forsyth hesitated. He'd wondered about that and couldn't decide.

"Shouldn't be difficult to find one," prompted the commander.

"What, you mean working for one of the villains?" joked Forsyth.

The commander's smile was strained: he was a breed of copper sensitive to that sort of comment. "I was thinking more of security firms and the like."

"I don't know," said Forsyth. "I'll see how things go for a while first."

The commander nodded and there was a pause. Seeing no reason for prolonging matters, Forsyth took the rest of the sherry at a gulp. But the commander had found a new topic of conversation.

"You've been around this part of London for most of your career, haven't you?"

"All of it. Except for a spell in Gravesend just after the war."

"And so what have been the biggest changes?"

Forsyth thought back and realised to his surprise he couldn't think of any. It'd always been the same: this overseeing of vice and violence, a job for a tough-minded saint that more often than not ended up being done by a soft-minded sinner.

"I don't think much has changed," he said. " 'Cept that the money's got bigger. And one or two things—drugs, videos." The commander's eyes were already dropping to the paperwork spread before him on the desk. So, all right he wasn't all that interested. All the same, he'd asked the question and was now going to get the answer whether he wanted it or not. "And I suppose there are more guns about. I mean with us as well as them. A lot more guns. But in other ways it's just the same as it ever was."

The commander gave a neutral smile and finished his own sherry.

"So now you'll be counting the days," he said.

"Yes, sir. I just hope they'll be quiet ones, that's all."

"So do I. And, if your interpretation of events is correct, then I don't see why they shouldn't be."

XII

Martyn returned a day earlier than he'd intended. Unbeknown to him, his parents had planned a short holiday in Cornwall to begin the day following their anniversary, so that he was faced with either staying alone in the house or making an early start back. He chose the early start and came up the M5 and M6 at a steady and effortless seventy.

It was certainly the quick way to travel, on the Suzuki, but it lacked the sense of adventure and infinite possibility that hitchhiking, his normal mode of transport, brought with it. For one thing, there was no one to talk to. He found himself crooning old pop songs and then rehearsing again and again in his head the scene that would be played when he arrived back at the bungalow.

For he was determined to leave. To arrive with the announcement of his departure on his lips. His few days away from Julie had given him time to think and loosened her spell over him. It was the loss of his job that'd changed everything and left him in an impossible position. He couldn't even pretend to be paying his way anymore. He was living in her bungalow and on her money; even riding on her bike.

How she'd react was anybody's guess. There were moments when he could see her not turning a hair. Others when he wondered if he'd get back to find she'd come to the same decision and was throwing him out even before he'd had the chance to tell her he was leaving. Though he somehow doubted it. Now that he knew her better, he'd seen beyond the wisecracking, classy bird, which was how she'd first appeared to him. He knew—and it depressed him to know—she was more vulnerable and less certain of herself than that.

It'd gone two o'clock in the afternoon when he finally left the motorway and began to thread his way along the minor roads that led to Coniston. By two-thirty he was coming up the track towards the bungalow. He pulled up before the front door and switched off the roaring engine.

He took off his helmet and stretched himself. Then he stepped up to the door, which was slightly ajar, and went in.

"Martyn . . . ?" Her call was hesitant, tentative. "Martyn, is that you?"

"Yes," he called back quickly, not wanting to alarm her. She, of course, couldn't be expecting him. How long should he leave it before telling her he was off again? Not too long, or he'd be seduced by her presence and by the memories of summer the bungalow contained.

She came hurrying to meet him. "Martyn," she said, and took his hand. "Thank God."

He'd been so preoccupied with his own misgivings it was a moment before he realised she was in a state of shock. Her eyes were wide and staring and she clung to his arm.

"What?" he said. "What's the matter?"

"Something's happened."

"What do you mean?"

"In the kitchen," she said dully.

He started forward, then had to wait for her to let go of his arm and step back to let him pass. The kitchen door was open and he looked in without having had time to think of what it might be or prepare himself for it.

There was a man lying on the floor. A large man who seemed to have fallen awkwardly. His face was against the tiled flooring and his left arm was bundled beneath him.

Martyn gave a grunt of surprise and moved towards the prostrate body. Some instinct kept him from touching it; instead, he leaned over it, looking for signs of life.

There didn't seem to be any. Only the protruding handle of a kitchen knife buried to its hilt in the man's stomach. There was a pool of blood on the floor below it.

Martyn straightened up abruptly and stepped back. Julie, moving as though in her sleep, had come into the kitchen behind him. He started to speak to her, then had to clear his throat before his voice would come.

"Is he . . . is he dead?"

"I don't know."

"Are you all right? I mean you're not hurt or anything?"

She shook her head.

He turned back to the inert figure and forced himself to place his fingers against its neck, feeling for the carotid artery. There was no pulse. The skin was warm only with a life that had already left it.

He straightened up slowly, then looked at Julie.

"Who did it? Who killed him?"

She started to shake her head. "I didn't . . . I didn't mean to. It was all . . . just horrible!" She clung to him. "Please, Martyn, please, I didn't mean to. It was all . . ."

He stopped her by pulling her to him and holding her in his arms.

"It's all right," he said gently. "It's all over."

"I thought he was going to kill me."

"Look, let's go into the lounge. Out of here."

She didn't seem able to move of her own accord so he had to take her by the arms and all but carry her into the lounge.

"Sit down."

"I'd like a drink," she said.

He went and picked up the brandy bottle but she said, "Whisky." He poured both of them a stiff whisky and came back to where she was propped up in a corner of the sofa.

"Did you . . . were you holding the knife?"

"Yes."

"Who is he?"

"I don't know."

"So what happened?"

She took a deep breath. He had the impression of someone resurfacing. She drained her glass and held it out to him.

"He was a thief," she said, while he went to get her a refill. "I found him in here. He'd just come in through the door. I said what are you doing, who are you? And then he hit me." There was a red weal on one side of her face. "He wanted the money. He wanted to know where I kept the money."

"And did you tell him?"

"I said it was in the kitchen. That was when he hit me again because he thought I was trying to be funny."

"He would."

"I told him I wasn't trying to be funny. And I took him in and showed him the money in the drawer. And it was when I did that I saw the knife. It was lying there on the draining board."

There was a long pause as she lit a cigarette.

"You picked it up," prompted Martyn gently.

"Yes." Then an outburst: "Well, he was a thief! And, I mean, he'd already hit me. I didn't know what he was going to do next. How could I?"

"No, it's all right," he comforted her.

"I thought he was going to kill me."

"It's all right," he urged, patting her hand and kissing her. "It wasn't your fault."

She slowly regained her composure. "I couldn't believe it when I heard the sound of the bike."

"I just wish I'd been earlier."

Once he felt it safe to leave her, he went back into the kitchen and looked again at the fallen figure. Now, knowing the man was dead, he had time to notice other things about him. He'd been in his early forties and was wearing a shirt, slacks and blouson top. There was a gold medallion round his neck and small tattoos of snakes on the back of each hand.

He returned to the lounge. It was time to act. They'd been petrified long enough by the horror of the situation.

"Have you rung anybody? Police or ambulance?"

She slowly shook her head.

"Don't worry," he said. "I'll do it."

He moved to the telephone but, before he could begin to dial, she was on her feet and clutching at him.

"No, don't, Martyn, please! Please let's not call the police."

She couldn't mean what she was saying. There was a dead man on the kitchen floor. She couldn't be suggesting they kept quiet about it?

"We'll have to do something," he said gently. Meaning inform the authorities.

"We can bury him. No one'll ever know."

He looked at her, dazed by the idea.

"They wouldn't," she urged. "I don't want the police, newspapers, all that. Please, Martyn."

He could only assume she was still in a state of shock. Certainly he couldn't do what she was asking. He picked up the phone and started to dial.

"No," she screamed. "What the hell do you think you're doing?"

"Ringing the police."

"Oh no, you're not!"

She grabbed the receiver from him, no longer imploring but vicious and determined. "What are you trying to do to me? I've told you, I don't want the police. I don't want all the publicity. Don't you think I've gone through enough as it is?"

He couldn't reply, not wanting to antagonise her further.

"Please, Martyn, help me," she pleaded.

He took a breath. "No," he said quietly. "I can't. And if you won't let me phone then I'll have to go down to the police station in town."

She gave a sigh and closed her eyes. He thought she'd given up but then, when she opened her eyes again, she said, "Sit down."

"Oh, come on . . ." he began to protest.

"Sit down," she ordered. The edge of hysteria had gone. She was still tense but was now controlled, meeting his gaze and daring him to defy her.

To appease her, he sat on the edge of a chair. He wanted her to understand that, say what she might, he was still intent on informing the police.

"He wasn't a burglar," she said quietly.

"What?"

"I said he wasn't a burglar. He'd come from London."

Her manner told him this was the truth; the other story had been lies.

"You know I said I used to work in London?"

He nodded.

"Well, when I said a model that was the truth, yes, but it wasn't exactly *Vogue* or *Harper's Bazaar* stuff."

He guessed what was coming before she said it.

"It was porn. Pornography. Hard, soft. Magazines, videos."

She waited for his reaction but he had none, neither of surprise nor outrage. Coming after the body in the kitchen with the knife in its guts, this was kids' stuff.

"Yes?"

"Oh, I didn't do it for long. I was clever enough at least to see that it was a mug's game. For the girls I mean. There's all the money in the world to be made if you're running it."

"So you started to run it . . . ?"

"I made sure I became the girlfriend of the man that did. And then the business partner."

"Congratulations," he muttered.

"I knew you wouldn't like it. I knew you'd be happier not knowing."

He'd have been happier, he thought, to have learned the truth under other circumstances, not as the postscript to a body on the kitchen floor.

"You've got to help me, Martyn. Please."

There was a silence. It was then he should have left. Gone and reported everything to the police. Staying was an admission he might help her after all.

"You still haven't told me who the man is."

She resumed the story. "I got involved in running the business. Well, various businesses actually. They weren't really illegal but not the sort of thing you get the Queen's Award for either."

"Porn?" he said, wanting to be sure.

"Yes. Imported mostly. Magazines from Holland, videos from the U.S. Even where it's been shot in this country in the first place it's safer to send it abroad for reproduction . . ."

"All right," he said, cutting her short. "So what happened?"

"Well, I told you about my friend. The one who was on heroin and who died. She was the reason I got out and came up here."

"So that part was true?"

She looked to see that he wasn't being sarcastic. "Yes. That part was true."

"Who owns the bungalow?"

"The firm. The business. Whatever you want to call it."

"And that's where all the money comes from?"

"Yes."

"And the man you killed . . . ?"

"There's been some trouble. A sort of gang warfare I suppose you might call it. Between two firms."

"One of which is yours."

"Yes. First one side has a go, then the other. The man in the kitchen—he was part of all that. He'd come to smash this place up. And me as well."

"He'd have . . . he'd have killed you?" asked Martyn, still struggling to get everything clear.

She shrugged. "I don't know. I just thank God I never found out."

"But the stabbing was in self-defence?" This he had to know above all else. Now that the moral landscape had clouded over, it was his single point of reference.

"Of course. I just grabbed the first thing. I mean how else could it have happened? You don't think I lured him here in order to kill him, do you?"

The absurdity of that reassured him. Whatever the bizarre and sordid background to the man's appearance at the bungalow, his death had come about from a desperate piece of self-defence by a woman scared out of her wits.

"I still don't see why we can't ring the police," he said cautiously. "I mean it would still be self-defence . . . accidental . . ."

"But they'd find out who he was," she objected. "They'd find out what he was doing here. It'd be all over the papers. Can't you see it? Ex-porno movie star involved in gangland killing."

Martyn hesitated. Suppose she was right? It still hardly added up to a reason for secretly disposing of the body . . . did it?

But she'd more to add.

"And you know what'd happen then, don't you?"

"What?"

"I'd be the next target. I'd have to be. The other side couldn't let it rest at that."

"You'd get police protection," he protested weakly.

"For how long? And what sort of a life would that be anyway?"

He couldn't answer. Nor could he continue to insist on informing the police. Not if it meant putting her own life at risk, having her end up skewered on somebody's kitchen floor.

There was a roll of heavy-duty polythene sheeting in a corner of the garage which had originally been the wrapping for a new mattress but would now do as a makeshift shroud for the body. They brought it into the open, shook the dust off it and then unrolled it so it was lying flat on the patio outside the French windows. Then, together, they went to attempt the daunting task of carrying out the dead bulk from the kitchen floor. Martyn was to take the shoulders and Julie the feet.

"One, two, three," he counted, and heaved the torso from the floor.

It was a movement that displaced the air from the lungs. The mouth opened and something between a sigh and a groan came out. Julie gave a scream and went rushing from the kitchen.

"For Christ's sake!" shouted Martyn, struggling alone with the corpse. "Come on!" He was on the edge and frightened they might be interrupted; certainly in no mood for female squeamishness.

She came back, biting her lip and apologising, but then found she could do no more than lift the feet a few inches from the floor. The body sagged between them.

"I'll drag it," gasped Martyn. "Let go."

That way, a few arduous feet at a time, he slid the ungainly weight across the kitchen tiles, bumped it across the lounge carpet and then out through the French windows. He'd begun by fastidiously keeping the dead man's face away from his own, then, becoming desperate and tired, ended in a near embrace.

"There's hardly any blood," reported Julie, following him out. "Except in the kitchen."

"Never mind that. Let's get him out of the way first," said Martyn, knowing they were still visible to anyone approaching the bungalow.

"What about the knife?" Julie asked. Then, while he was hesitating, she bent past him, gripped the handle with both hands and pulled with a gasp of effort. There was a small gurgle as it came.

"Well done," he muttered.

"I'll clean it," she said and, holding it away from her between thumb and forefinger, she took it inside.

On impulse, and keeping his eyes averted from the wound, Martyn made a quick check of the dead man's pockets. He found loose change, a bunch of keys, cigarettes and lighter and a railway timetable. Then a wallet which contained forty or fifty pounds in notes, a Barclaycard, some printed cards that seemed to be passes to clubs and the return half of a rail ticket to Euston. The name on the Barclaycard was "R. Senior."

He replaced everything, straightened the body as best he could, then hurriedly began to fold the polythene around it. Sellotape was all they'd been able to find with which to fasten it. The polythene was a few inches short so that the feet stuck out at the bottom. Martyn had to kneel on it to hold it in place as, breaking the Sellotape with his teeth, he managed to stick the whole parcel together.

He worked with a desperate speed, muttering to himself, urging himself on. "Come on, that's it. Now that . . ." It wasn't just the fear of discovery but also the fear that if he looked too closely at what he was doing he'd be unable to continue. When he'd first said to Julie, "All right, I'll help you," she'd rushed to embrace him, full of gratitude, but he'd pushed her away, insisting they got on with it without delay. It was the only way—take it at a run and don't look down.

Julie came back out of the house.

"I've got the blood off."

"All of it?"

"Yes."

They stood looking at the wrapped body.

"He was called Senior," he said.

It seemed to mean nothing to her. "Oh?"

"He came by train."

"Well, he's going by car," she said. "It's the only way we're ever going to shift him."

She reversed the Porsche round from the front of the house so that it approached the patio boot first. As it arrived, Martyn dropped to one knee and struggled to lift the body. It was easier now it was wrapped. It'd ceased to be repulsive or to deserve dignity; he could now lug it about as he would a sack of potatoes.

Folded double, it fitted easily into the boot. They both felt relieved when Martyn was at last able to slam down the lid and it was out of sight.

"Better make sure we haven't overlooked anything," he said, waving a vague hand at the ground. They shuffled around, staring down for what could later on be damning evidence—a bloodstain or some human hairs—but found nothing.

Martyn, still on edge, walked around the gardens of the bungalow, then up and down the lane outside. Wanting to explore further, he went back for his bike and rode for several miles in each direction. But there was no sign of a car left parked or one in which an accomplice might be sitting waiting. Had the dead man been alone then? And had he approached on foot or by taxi?

Julie couldn't help. She'd been aware of the man only when he'd been there in the house with her.

"How long was all this before I arrived back?"

She wasn't sure. "Five or ten minutes perhaps."

An elderly couple in a Morris Marina were the only people he could remember passing as he'd approached the bungalow from town. The man had probably been alone then. And possibly on foot. Though, more likely, he'd taken a taxi from town and dismissed it while still some distance from the bungalow.

Obviously a man intent on violence and destruction had good reason for covering his tracks and would have arrived as inconspicuously as possible. It was unlikely that anyone would notice his failure to depart.

The site for burial was Martyn's idea.

"We want somewhere that's sheltered," Julie said as they sat drinking coffee. "So we can dig without anybody seeing us."

"It always looks so obvious though, doesn't it."

"What does?"

"When the ground's been dug over. It takes years before it looks normal again."

He had to put down his cup as his hand began to tremble uncontrollably. He still couldn't believe in any of this: the wrapping up of the body as though it were a dead dog and now this callous discussion of how best to dispose of it. Least of all could he believe they'd ever get away with it.

"Would it help if it were somewhere wet?" asked Julie.

It was then the idea came to him.

"There's a place near the caravan. It's a sort of copse with trees and bushes and there's a stream runs through it. Only the stream's dried up. It's been that way for most of the summer." She frowned, not following, so he added, "It's not going to stay that way for much longer, is it. It's got to rain soon."

"Tomorrow."

"What?"

"It said on the forecast. It's going to rain tomorrow."

He held out his hands in a gesture that said: what more could they want?

"If we bury him in the bed of that stream then, by the time it's been raining for an hour or two, any signs of our digging will have been washed away."

"Suppose it washes too much away and exposes the body?"

"No." He waved the objection aside. "We'll go much too deep for that." Only the gruesomeness of the idea restrained his enthusiasm.

"All right, if you think so," said Julie, not too keen but with nothing to offer in its place.

They sat around the bungalow until nine o'clock that evening, making occasional forays to check they weren't being watched and on one occasion opening the boot of the car and peering in to still Julie's fear that the body was alive and struggling to free itself from its polythene shroud. It'd gone dark by the time they left. Julie drove with unusual caution. She was wearing a pair of yellow Wellingtons while Martyn made do with his old trainers. He took with him a spade and a garden fork found in one of the outhouses. They followed the road that took them to the spot below Martyn's caravan where she'd parked on the night of the summer storm. It was as near as they could get, though still a good hundred-and-fifty yards from the trees that would hide them.

They got out of the car. Julie took charge of the spade and fork and then, risking everything, they opened the boot and Martyn heaved the body out onto his shoulder. Immediately it was balanced, he set off in a stumbling run across the field, leaving Julie to shut up the car and follow him.

It was a back-breaking business, this dash through the gloom, always fearing the ground would betray him with a pothole or rut and send him headlong with the body on top of him. In the end he staggered twice but managed to avoid going down. Once safe inside the cover of the trees, he dumped the body unceremoniously and stood gasping to get his breath back. His heart was pounding and his forehead wet with perspiration.

It was a few minutes before Julie arrived, walking carefully and carrying the spade and garden fork.

"Did you see him?" she hissed.

"See who?"

"The cyclist. The one who went past in the road."

He could only look at her. He'd been so preoccupied with his own journey that he'd no conception of what might have been going on behind him.

"You'd set off across the field," she said. "And he came up and stopped. Asked me if I wanted any help."

"Did he see me?"

"I don't think so."

"What did you say?"

"I said no. That I was all right. And so he went."

"Well, as long as he didn't see anything . . ."

"He saw the spade and fork. He must have done."

They stood in silence, absorbing the truth of that. Though it was too late now to do anything other than to get on with it.

"Where's the body?" whispered Julie.

"Here," he said, and prodded it with his foot so she could hear the crackle of the polythene. Now they were beneath the trees the darkness was almost total.

"And where's the stream?"

He took her hand and led her the few yards to it. At first it was no more than a hollow they could feel with their feet and then, as their eyes grew accustomed to the dark, they saw the dried-up bed, full of small stones and dust.

"You see what I mean," urged Martyn. "The first time it rains, all this top surface'll be moved down and there'll be no sign of any digging."

They brought the body further into the copse and then, using the spade, Martyn marked out an area that was about six feet long and two feet across and fitted neatly inside the existing course of the stream.

"Can I do anything?" she said.

"You can act as lookout. Let me know if anybody shows an interest."

"OK," she said, gave him a quick, encouraging kiss and moved away.

First he used the fork to loosen the earth, and then the spade to excavate what he had loosened. It was easy to begin with and he made quick work of the top foot or so of earth and stones. Then, going deeper, he found the earth to be criss-crossed by the trailing roots of the nearby trees. At first these were no more than thin, wispy extremities that had crept up to near the surface and were easily pushed aside or sliced with the spade. Then, lower still, the roots became more substantial and he had to stop his digging and use the spade like an axe, hacking at them until they were cut through and could be pulled out.

He was down to the depth of three feet, a little more in places, before he stopped to rest, wishing now they'd thought of bringing something to drink. Hearing the work stop, Julie found her way back to him from where she was on lookout.

"Have you done it?"

He shook his head. "Having a rest."

"I'll go back on watch then, shall I?"

"You'd better."

They exchanged another kiss and she moved away, back to her post. He looked at the luminous face of his watch: it was after ten. Despite his exertions, he began to feel the night chill through his shirt.

How much further down should he go? When bodies were discovered, the newspapers invariably spoke of them as being in "shallow graves" as though the murderer had betrayed himself by skimping on the job. Another two foot at least, vowed Martyn. And never mind if it took until early morning.

Now it was more cutting and hacking than digging. He would mark off a small square in his mind's eye, then drive the sharp edge of the spade again and again into it until the protruding roots had been pulverised and could be shovelled out. All that he removed he tried to keep to a single pile at the side of the hole since he foresaw that it was around the hole—and not above it where the water would do the job for him—that the signs of his labours would be most difficult to obliterate.

He was so preoccupied he didn't notice Julie's return until she was standing at his shoulder and trying to speak to him.

"What?" he asked, stopping work, fearing she'd seen someone approaching.

"Rain," she said. "It's started raining."

He looked down in alarm, as if expecting to see a small tidal wave sweeping down the streambed towards them. Now he'd stopped digging, he could hear the water hitting the leaves. Here beneath the trees they were dry and he could continue, but how long before the stream would reappear, flooding the intended grave and making burial impossible?

"Isn't this deep enough?" she said peering into the dark hole.

He took the decision. "Yes," he said. "It'll have to be."

A shallow grave, he thought. Well, it wasn't all that shallow. Certainly four feet.

"Keep out of the way," he warned her.

He pushed his arms under the body in order to lift it but the digging must have weakened him and it felt as though it were bolted to the earth. He'd have to roll it, pushing rather than lifting. The body turned, its protruding feet showing that it was first on its back, now on its face. Still it wasn't quite in line with the hole. He gripped one end of the polythene covering and manoeuvred it until it was lying parallel. Then another push. It rolled over the edge and hit the bottom with a thump.

It was such a perfect fit that, under other circumstances, he might have given a small cheer of triumph.

"Right," he gasped. "Now all this back on top."

Julie stayed to help him, using the fork while he used the spade. Within what seemed like seconds after the hard labour of removing it, half the earth had been pushed back in. As the body disappeared, he began to believe that they might, after all, get away with it.

"Wait a minute," he said, stopping her.

He jumped into the grave and began stamping on the loose earth, refusing to think about what he might be doing to the body beneath. He went up and down the length of the trench until satisfied it was packed as hard as he could get it.

Then they shovelled in what was left. It was barely enough to bring the surface back to its former level, which was odd considering the bulk of the body that'd been added. He used the fork to rake the ground around them, hoping to hide the signs of their presence. At last they seemed to have finished.

They stood for a moment. The rain was now a steady drumming on the leaves above and odd drips of water were beginning to find their way through.

"Can we go?" asked Julie softly.

"Yes," he said, and gathered up the spade and fork.

They came out from under the trees and were surprised by the cold gusts of rain that sent them hurrying back to the car. Julie seemed to have rediscovered her taste for fast driving and had them back at the bungalow in no time. They made no attempt to clean up the car or even remove the spade and fork from the boot but went inside, eager for a drink and something to eat. They found some bread in the kitchen and made sandwiches, then finished off what remained of the coffee. Finding his hands and clothes caked with dirt, Martyn went into the bathroom for a shower.

"I'm going to bed." Julie's voice came to him through the door. "See you tomorrow, OK?"

It surprised him that she should take the opportunity to slip away from him like that. Still, it was her privilege if she didn't want them to spend the night together.

Finishing his shower, he saw the light was still on in her room. The whisky bottle had gone from the lounge. It wasn't that she was sleeping then; probably more that she needed time to come to terms with things. He didn't disturb her but climbed the ladder to his own bed in the attic room.

He awoke at seven-fifteen the following morning and remembered instantly all that had happened the previous day. Overriding all else was a feeling of amazement he could have played a part in such horrors and survived them.

Knowing he wouldn't get back to sleep, he got out of bed, put on some clothes and went outside. Everywhere was still wet from last night's downpour. A pool of water had gathered below the level of the patio.

On an impulse he started off out of the garden and into the lane down which Julie had driven them last night. In the eyes of the world he was going for his early morning jog; under cover of which he'd check on how far their plans had succeeded.

The thought that disaster might have struck already grew with every step. He was tormented by an image of rainwater, in torrential flood, tearing at the earth and revealing first an arm, then a head and then the whole body, which would then be carried off downstream for all to see.

It was a relief to arrive at the field and find it deserted but for a flock of scavenging gulls that arose at his approach. There were no police cars. No areas cordoned off by red tape. He trotted across the field, hesitated only a moment, and went into the copse. The stream had reestablished itself and was running merrily. Not a torrent that might reopen the earth but a steady flow, enough to obliterate all signs of last night's digging.

Pleased by all that he saw, Martyn returned to the bungalow with a lighter step. While in the mood for it, he'd clean out the car. He took the spade and fork and wiped each free of earth.

He came into the kitchen, looking for water to use on the car, and was startled to find Julie already there, looking pale and in her dressing gown.

"Morning," she said, and came to him for a kiss.

"I've been for a run," he told her. "So I went up to the field. Had a look to see how the stream was getting on."

She looked at him anxiously so that he hurried to reassure her.

"It's all right. There's no sign."

"We're going to be all right then?"

Why not, he thought. There must have been others who'd done it—killed and never been discovered.

"Yes," he said. "I think we are."

XIII

For Martyn the sense of horror at what they'd done grew rather than diminished in the days that followed. The suspense also grew. Would the man Senior be missed? Would the body be discovered? And could either the disappearance of the man or the reappearance of the body be traced back to himself and Julie? Worst of all was his realisation that any police officer worth his salt would see the burying of a polythene-wrapped body late at night as the aftermath not of an accidental killing but of murder, and that any jury of twelve average men and women wouldn't have too much of a problem in agreeing.

All he could do was try and put the business behind him, hope the stream would hide their tracks and the body never be discovered. The one thing he couldn't do was leave. Whatever resolutions he'd returned with from Bristol, he'd now committed himself to seeing things through alongside Julie. What they'd done that night had retied their lives together in a way that wouldn't easily be loosened.

In fact Julie seemed to recover before he did. Not for a second could he forget the body lying there beneath the earth and the stream. It was always in his consciousness, whether lingering behind other thoughts or projecting itself to the fore, making his face damp with perspiration and his hands tremble. Julie was calmer, more able to concentrate on the ordinary things of life. Barely forty-eight hours after the killing she was using the kitchen knife she'd pulled from the corpse to slice salami for lunchtime sandwiches.

She saw his nervousness and tried to reassure him.

"Nobody's enquired about him, have they. There's been nothing in the papers. I think we've got away with it. Don't you?"

"No," he said stubbornly, then hurried to add, "Oh, I don't

mean for any particular reason. It's just I can't believe anybody can do what we've done and get away with it."

"Oh yes, they can," she said softly. "And they have. Believe me, it happens all the time."

He did believe her, and wondered what sort of life she must have had to speak with such authority and take what had happened in her stride.

"Listen, Martyn," she said, putting her hands over his. "That man came here to burn this house down, perhaps even kill me and . . . well, I don't know what."

"I know," he said, "I'm not blaming you . . ."

"What I'm saying is," she said, stopping him, "he would have made damn sure nobody knew he was coming here."

"I suppose so."

"So whoever misses him—if anybody ever does—won't know where to even start looking. They certainly won't go to the police. The sort of people they are, that's the last thing they'd do. The body's well hidden. Even if, through some freak, it ever were discovered, there's nothing to connect it to us."

"I know," he admitted. "I know all that."

"Well then—we've got away with it."

He gave a reluctant assent. "We probably have."

"Then stop looking so worried," she said, gave him a kiss and went back to watching television.

He felt like objecting: it's easy for you—you're used to it. Everything about his own background and upbringing protested they must be punished for what they'd done. Yet here they were, watching television and eating salami sandwiches, while the body they'd buried was safely tucked away beneath sod and stream. It raised all manner of uneasy questions. How much of a charade was all this law-and-order business? How many other bodies lay around the country in various holes and corners? According to Julie—quite a lot.

Some four days after the killing (like the coming of Christ, it had given them a new calendar, becoming the moment from which all else was dated), they were eating in the Rockingham when, encouraged by the wine, he asked her to tell him more about her life in London. It was a topic that hadn't been mentioned by either of them since she'd blurted out the truth about her involvement in pornography.

"What do you want to know?"

He shrugged. "Whatever you want to tell me. Unless you'd rather not talk about it at all, in which case forget I ever asked."

"No, I don't mind," she said, though she'd already become more guarded and was eyeing him as if trying to assess just what it was he was after. "Like I said, I started off as a model. In magazines. Nudes. All that."

"How did you get into it?"

"I answered an ad in a newspaper. Models wanted, that sort of thing."

"And then you found out what it really was?"

"I knew all along," she said flatly. "I went into it with my eyes open. As well as my legs."

"You said films as well?"

"Yes. Blue movies. Hard porn I suppose you'd call them now, though this was, what, late sixties, early seventies when they just got referred to as 'dirty.' "

"I see."

He shifted uneasily, not sure just how to ask or what it was he wanted to know.

"You want to know what it was like?"

"Yes," he admitted, surprised to find that he did.

She laughed, took a sip of her drink, then said, "It varied. Sometimes you could kid yourself you were in real films, Hollywood and all that. But mostly it was like being meat in a butcher's window. And I'll tell you the worst part, shall I?"

"What?"

"The worst part was the men. The ones we had to . . . act with."

"Ah."

"God knows why, after they'd been as choosy as hell about the girls they wanted—I mean it was as though it was going to be some great epic the way they'd go through twenty or thirty girls before choosing one—so God knows why after all that they'd settle for the first fat, slobby, sweaty male that walked through the door. Which is why most of us preferred working with other girls." And, in case he wasn't clear just what she was getting at, she added mockingly, "I mean appearing in scenes that were what you might call exclusively female."

She was back to her old ways, he realised. She was teasing him, offering the juicy tidbit to see how he'd respond. Well, he'd respond by ignoring it.

"But you got out of all that."

"No."

He looked at her in surprise.

"I didn't get out," she said. "I simply got to the top."

"Was it that easy?"

"Yes. If you had the looks and were prepared to pay the price. Being available. Sleeping around."

He nodded dumbly. She smiled, not at all put out; in fact, apparently enjoying the opportunity to reminisce.

"I became the boss's girlfriend. Then wormed my way into the business side so that I was something more than just a pretty face."

"You became indispensable."

"More or less. Till I decided to dispense with myself."

And that seemed to be the end of it as the waiter arrived to collect their plates, and they were distracted by the business of ordering dessert and coffee. But then, when he'd moved away, she took up the topic again.

"Most of the girls were so dumb. Well, they still are. And those that aren't quite as dumb as the rest, they're apathetic, they've given up. They expect so little that they're grateful for anything. Even for the fact that someone wants to stick a camera halfway up their arse."

The waiter came with her ice cream but she pushed it to one side and went on talking. She was more earnest now and not teasing.

"But when you're part of the firm that's running all that—part of the organisation—well then, that's different. And how. You feel superior to the whole wide bloody world. See, you've got these stupid women working for you—tarts, models, dancers—who'll let themselves be herded around like sheep and used like lumps of meat and be kicked around and underpaid and still come back for more."

Martyn had to raise a warning finger to his lips as her voice had risen and was attracting the attention of those around them.

"And then, on the other hand," she went on, speaking more quietly, "there's the punters. The men. Believe it or not, they're even more stupid than the girls you've got working for you. So long as you're offering 'em sex of one sort or another—doesn't matter how bloody pathetic it is—they can be staring through a keyhole at some bird stripping or standing in a basement watching blurred videos—doesn't matter what it is, they'll pay and they'll keep paying and they'll never complain. The berks."

She stopped to light a cigarette.

"And you're in the middle making the money," said Martyn.

"And how. And I mean you really do feel that everybody's so stupid for letting you do it. Obviously the cops keep you on your toes, but they're happy enough providing nobody's stepping out of line. So you've got stupid tarts and stupid punters. In the end you decide that they deserve one another and leave 'em to it."

"You didn't have any conscience about it?" he asked.

"No. Like I say, they deserve it. And you're there running it. Pulling the strings. Playing God. It's a hard habit to kick."

He knew what she meant. For all the fear the buried body had caused him, it had brought him also a faint taste of that thrill she was talking about. It'd taken him to the threshold of the underworld. There was a kind of privilege to that as well as danger.

Two weeks after the killing Julie suddenly announced she'd be going out that evening and that, for once, she'd be going out alone.

"All right," he said, surprised but not offended.

"It's nothing for you to worry about. And I shouldn't be too late."

Her eagerness to reassure struck him as odd. They'd neither of them been in the habit of accounting for their every move. Why should she now feel a need to explain?

"Have a good time," he said to her when she came out of her bedroom, freshly made up and casually dressed in jeans and sweater.

"Oh, it's only somebody I have to see," she said, as though it were a chore to be gone through.

He stayed where he was in the lounge, listening to Bessie Smith on his headphones and reading Evelyn Waugh's *Officers and Gentlemen* which he'd bought that afternoon at a jumble sale in town. Normally he'd have gone to the door to see her off but he sensed that such attentions wouldn't be welcome on this occasion.

He lifted off his headphones and called out, "Bye."

To his surprise she was in the kitchen and not in the hallway on her way out as he'd thought. He heard a drawer being closed.

"Bye," she responded.

After she'd gone, he resisted as long as he could—about ten minutes—before his curiosity got the better of him. He put down his book, took off his headphones and went into the kitchen. Even then, he told himself it was a betrayal of her trust and a cheap trick. Undeniable, yet it didn't stop him going to the drawer where she kept the money and opening it.

A lot of the money was gone. He didn't know how much—they were both in the habit of taking whatever they needed without keeping any kind of accounts—but he'd have guessed that the missing amount was close to two thousand pounds. Why on earth should she have taken such a sum with her?

Of course it was her money and she could do with it as she pleased. She didn't have to consult or inform him. Though telling himself this didn't make it any the less of a mystery. Or any easier to ignore, coming as it did in the wake of the last, bloodier mystery that same kitchen had provided.

He went to bed around midnight but lay awake until he heard her car approach and pull up. The front door was opened and closed, then she was below him, moving around between lounge and kitchen. The television set was switched on—then off again. The last sound he heard was the closing of her bedroom door.

The following morning he was up first as usual and, confident he wouldn't be interrupted—she seldom appeared before ten— he went to the kitchen and checked the drawer. It was the same as last night: the two thousand pounds hadn't been replaced. Had it all gone then? Had she, in a single night, spent or given away or otherwise lost a small fortune in new ten-pound notes?

He closed the drawer. He couldn't ask her. Only hope she might tell him. Perhaps it was a loan to a friend. (But who?) Or the repayment of a debt. (Again—to whom?)

Or perhaps she was being blackmailed by someone who knew about the killing and had threatened to expose her to the police unless she coughed up. Which would also explain her self-conscious insistence on going alone. It was a farfetched and alarming idea but the only one he could think of that fitted the facts.

XIV

She made no reference to the night out, neither to where she'd been nor whom she'd been with, until Martyn couldn't resist asking, "Everything all right last night?"

"Yes," she said, managing a note of surprise as if it were already ancient history.

She was having a late breakfast of yoghurt and fruit juice, a healthy beginning to a diet that would end the day with alcohol and tobacco.

He persevered. "Go anywhere nice?"

This time she looked at him and said firmly, "Please don't ask me about it, Martyn. I thought I made it clear it was private."

"You did," he said. And, since that seemed to put an end to that, he left her and wandered out into the garden where there were already leaves falling and plants and flowers in need of pruning.

Still, it was a fine, clear day; he decided to take the bike and head westwards for the coast. Julie seemed set for a day of slobbing round the bungalow and would be best left.

"Do you want me to do any shopping?" he asked as he buckled on his leathers before setting off.

"Up to you," she said. "I haven't a clue."

She was about as domestic as a fox. He'd asked the question only to reestablish communications between them.

He rode out over the high fells that were to the south of the Old Man of Coniston, then into the fells beyond that unrolled until eventually they reached the sea. It was a landscape that buckled into giant dips and rises before him and on which sheep seemed to be everywhere, penned in by the dry-stone walls that ran in crazed patterns about the hillsides. Away from the tourist areas and with the summer gone, Martyn felt an intruder in a landscape that seemed determined to ignore him.

By early afternoon he'd reached the coast, a bleak expanse of windswept sands, uninhabited but for warning notices that told him to keep off. The Irish Sea beyond looked grey and uninviting.

He sat a while before starting back. Some expectant gulls wheeled in and then, disappointed, glided away again.

Suppose he didn't go back at all but carried on, north or south, till he came to another temporary alighting point that would see him through the next bit of his life? Julie wouldn't be all that surprised, would she? She was certainly capable of surviving alone and for all he knew might welcome the sudden break as much as he would.

So, let that be it then. He wouldn't go back, but would carry on up the coast and see where it led him.

"No chance," he said aloud, and hauled the bike round so it was facing inland. It was only a game, all this supposing, and he'd be back in Coniston within a couple of hours. The prospect puzzled and dismayed him. From being master of his own fate, he'd become enmeshed in a web of circumstances from which there seemed little chance of escape. It would have been difficult enough leaving Julie after the summer they'd shared; then had come the body on the kitchen floor and the nightmare of carting off and burying it, all of which had kept him at the bungalow at least until the outcome were certain; and now, just as he might have believed they'd got away with it and he might therefore think of moving on, there was this strange affair of the disappearing money to postpone still further his plans for leaving.

He set off back, climbing into the hills and away from the flat coastline. He'd solve nothing by staring out to sea or looking at sheep. What he had to do was talk to Julie. Approach her directly and demand to know what the hell was going on. It may have been her money, fair enough, and she may therefore have the right to do with it as she pleased; but it was his neck that'd be in the noose alongside hers if it were a matter of blackmail and she should mishandle it.

He arrived back in Coniston for five-thirty, tired from the trip and just in time to catch the supermarket where he picked up a loaf of bread and some groceries. He returned to his bike to find someone waiting for him.

"I thought it was you under all that leather," she said. "You're looking very macho these days."

It was Wendy Harriman, though now with her hair cut short, punk style, and a leather thong tied round her forehead.

"Hi, Wendy," he said. "How're you?" He thought about his caravan and its broken windows. Too late now of course to start asking if she knew anything about it.

"OK," she said. "Haven't see you around though."

"No, well. The boat job finished so I don't get into town much."

"I love the bike."

"Not bad is it."

He realised he was glad to see her and to stand chatting idly. If he did have one foot in the underworld then it was good to feel the other still on terra firma.

"And what're you doing with yourself?" he asked.

"Oh, still waitressing."

"At the Lake View?"

"Where else? Don't know how much longer I'll be able to stick it though." There was a pause, then she said, "Look, how about letting me buy you a drink? For old times' sake."

His first, automatic reaction was to look for an excuse, then he checked himself. Why should he? Wasn't part of his problem the way he'd made Julie not only the centre but virtually the sole occupant of his world?

"All right," he said. "You're on."

The pubs had just opened for the evening. They went into the Crown Hotel which had hand pumps and a coal fire. He ordered a pint of bitter and Wendy asked for the same.

"I thought about you last night," she said, when they'd sat at a small circular table with iron legs that competed uncomfortably with their own.

"Did you? Why?"

"Oh, I was working. In the restaurant at the hotel. And that lady friend of yours came in."

Martyn was taken completely by surprise. Wendy gave a little smile, pleased at her success. He thought, she's been hanging around all day hoping to see me. There's nothing accidental about this meeting.

When he didn't reply, she said. "The lady with the Porsche."

"Yes."

"She was with a man. Do you know him?"

"No," said Martyn, then wished he'd lied and said yes.

"Ah," she said. "Sorry. Hope I haven't put my foot in it."

"No," he said evenly. "I knew she was meeting someone. Only it was to do with business. Someone I don't know. All right?"

"All right by me," she said tartly.

They talked about other things—auditions she'd been to, news of mutual acquaintances—managing to keep the conversation going while they finished their drinks. Now that he'd got over her surprise announcement about seeing Julie, Martyn was curious to know more—though reluctant to give Wendy the satisfaction of admitting it.

"That man you saw Julie with last night," he said.

"Yes?"

"You don't happen to know his name, do you?"

She looked at him. "I thought you said it was just business."

"It was," he said. "I'd still be very grateful if you could tell me his name."

He could see she didn't believe him, but did that matter? This was life and death, not some lovers' tiff.

"I could find out," she said.

"How?"

"He stayed overnight in the hotel. I can get his name from reception."

"But no one would know . . . ?"

"No! the receptionist's a pal of mine. She'll let me have a look at his card. No problem."

"You're sure?"

"Positive. Shall I give you a ring?"

He thought quickly about the possible problems and said, "Well why don't I come up and see you at the hotel?"

She jumped at the idea. "Sure. I'm there every evening apart from Sundays and alternate Mondays."

Perhaps it was what she'd been angling for all along, some kind of liaison between them. So what though? He needed an ally if anyone did.

"Thanks," he said and suddenly, impulsively, gave her a kiss on the cheek as they rose to depart. She looked up at him with shining eyes and he thought, oh, no, please don't get the wrong idea. Life's complicated enough at the moment without that.

They went out of the pub together.

"I'll ask as soon as I get back," she said. "So you could call in tonight if you liked."

"I'm not sure just when," he said evasively. "Sometime this week though."

He wanted to ask her more about Julie's mystery companion but felt he'd already gone as far as he could. Any further and she'd sense there was something odd going on.

Fortunately she supplied him, unbidden, with everything he wanted.

"I thought they seemed a peculiar couple," she said. "You know, not like a pair that're on a night out."

He managed a chuckle. "Really?"

"Well, he was younger than she was. No more than twenty, twenty-one, something like that. And they were arguing all the time."

"I told you it was business."

"Well, I don't know what it was. Only that they were arguing. I mean you can't help noticing when you're serving somebody."

But what about? Martyn desperately wanted to ask. Did you hear what they were arguing about? But she seemed to have no more to tell him and they parted, he on his bike heading out of town and she on foot making for the hotel above it.

He knew Julie wouldn't take kindly to being questioned, but it had to be now or never.

"There's something I must know about last night," he said when once he'd got back in the bungalow and got rid of the shopping.

"I've told you, I don't want to talk about it."

"Well, I do."

"Oh yes?"

She stood facing him, hands on hips. She was in a foul mood, already out for a row.

"I want to know if there's anything going on. I mean anything wrong."

"And what makes you think there might be?"

"You took an awful lot of money out with you."

Her tone was icy. "And how would you know that?"

"I looked in the drawer."

"Oh, did you . . . !"

"I'm sorry."

"You might well be sorry. Sneaking around, spying on me behind my back. Well, at least I know what I have to do in future. Keep everything locked up. That's what I have to do, is it?"

"I just want to know if there's anything wrong," he said stubbornly.

"And what gives you the right to know?"

"Well, for one thing . . ." he began, but she wasn't interested in his answer and swept on over him.

"By what right do you go sneaking around this house, checking up on what I'm doing? And, most of all what bloody right do you think you've got to start telling me what I should and shouldn't do with my own money?"

"I'm not trying to tell you . . ."

"Because you know what I ought to tell you?" When he didn't answer she repeated, "You know what I ought to tell you?"

"No," he said quietly.

"I ought to tell you to get the hell out of here. And that's exactly what I am going to tell you if you carry on questioning me about what I'm doing in my own time and with my own money."

Martyn sighed. He'd little hope of a straight answer while she ranted on like this.

"Can we start again?" he said.

"Can we what?"

"Can we start this conversation again?"

She gave a sarcastic laugh. "You can do what the hell you like."

"I didn't come back here wanting to have a row with you."

"I'm glad to hear it."

"And I didn't come back wanting to pry into your private life."

"I'm glad to hear that, too."

"But there's something I've got to ask you." She stood stony-faced and said nothing, which he took as permission to continue. "When you were out last night you took a lot of money with you."

"Is that the question?"

"No."

"Then what is it, this thing you want to know?"

"Please, Julie . . ."

"I'm listening."

He tried again. "After you'd gone out last night I looked in the kitchen drawer and it seemed to me that you'd taken a lot of money with you. Must have been close to two thousand pounds." She made not the slightest gesture to confirm or deny his estimate. "Now, all right, I know that it's your money. And I know that I've no right to even look in that drawer."

"I'm still waiting to hear what it is you want to know."

"Well, let me tell you what I don't want to know first."

"Oh, for Christ's sake!" To demonstrate her impatience, she went and poured herself a drink, then lit a cigarette to go with it.

"I don't want to know where you went . . ."—something of a cheat this, since Wendy had already told him—"and I don't want to know who you were with . . ."—something else that Wendy was in the process of digging up for him, but anyway—"all I want to know is, did last night and that money have anything to do with what happened here two weeks ago?"

She appeared at first to be ignoring his question, pacing up and down and sipping at her drink. Then she said, "I see."

"Because if it does have anything to do with that then it most certainly does concern me. If it doesn't . . . well then, you're quite right: it's your business and I've no right to ask anything about it."

"Well, it doesn't."

"It doesn't . . . ?"

"Doesn't have anything to do with what happened."

"Honestly?"

"Cross my heart," she said, "and hope to die."

He went to her and gave her a quick, apologetic kiss. "I'm sorry about looking in the drawer. Only once I'd done that then I had to ask. You can see that, can't you?"

"No," she said. "But I'll forgive you anyway."

"Thanks."

It was an immense relief to learn the money hadn't gone to pay off some blackmailer. As long as he could be sure of that, he couldn't care less where else it might have ended up.

"In fact," she said, "I'll tell you what I did last night, shall I?"
He hesitated. "You don't have to."

"I know I don't have to. I wouldn't be telling you if I had."

"Well, all right then."

"Last night," she said, "I went out with an old school friend. A girlfriend. And she's in a mess. I'm sure you won't want me to go into details but she needed to borrow some money without her husband or anybody knowing. So I helped her out. Happy now?"

His heart sank as she spoke. Set alongside what he already knew, what she was giving him had to be a pack of lies from start to finish. It wasn't a case of whether Julie or Wendy was the more honest and reliable; simply that Wendy had nothing to gain by lying and Julie had. Wendy's account of Julie's stormy evening with her dining companion who was male and in his early twenties had the clear ring of unsolicited truth about it. The fiction that Julie had so glibly trotted out was then only a depressing confirmation of all his earlier fears.

"What's the matter?" she said, looking at him. "You don't believe me?"

"Julie, love . . ."

"I said don't you believe me?"

"Not entirely, no."

"Why?"

He couldn't say why, could only shake his head and shrug.

"So you're calling me a liar? Well, thank you very much. You sneak around the house, you spy on me and now you're calling me a liar! Well, if you feel like that then why don't you just piss off out of here! Go on. Piss off out of here if that's what you think." She threw the glass she was holding. It bounced across the carpet, splattering it with whisky. "Go on, get out. I don't ever want to talk to you again."

She turned and made for the door, then paused, made a small detour that allowed her to grab the whisky bottle and her packet of cigarettes, then stalked out of the lounge and into the hallway. There was a crash as she slammed her bedroom door behind her.

He made no move to stop her. She'd told him everything he wanted to know. It was as good as a confession, all that invention about the girlfriend when once she thought she'd allayed his fears and then all the blustering and shouting when she saw he hadn't believed her. Clearly he'd been right all along. Somebody knew about the killing and was putting the screws on her.

He ran his hands through his hair and gave a groan of dismay. He couldn't abandon her: he knew too much for that and cared too much for her. Yet he knew too little to set about helping her. And he wasn't going to get to know any more from her, not anyway while she was in this mood.

Perhaps he'd go back into town then. Go and see Wendy and see what more he could learn.

He left the bike and walked, wanting time to think. Dusk was encroaching and with it a chilling wind. He thrust his hands into his pockets and strode along under the trees.

Reaching the town, he stopped at a café for something to eat and to give Wendy time to complete her enquiries. There was, he supposed, some kind of dreadful consolation to be got from knowing that things were as bad as they could be. Nor had he much in the way of alternatives. He had to find out who was behind this and take whatever steps were necessary to rescue both himself and Julie from the blackmailer's clutches. He wondered how far he'd be prepared to go.

Arriving at the Lake View Hotel, he found it brightly lit for an evening of wining and dining. He went and stood at the cocktail bar, feeling out of place and refusing the menu that was offered him.

Wendy was presumably in the restaurant. He went to its entrance, hoping to spot her, but couldn't. He returned to the bar and ordered a drink.

"Do you know Wendy Harriman?" he asked the barman. "I think she works here."

He nodded. "Waitress in the restaurant."

"Do you know if she's on tonight?"

"Who shall I say wants her?"

He gave his name and waited as the barman went to a telephone at the back of the bar and spoke into it. A minute later Wendy arrived in a uniform of white blouse and black skirt.

"Well, you don't waste much time."

"No," he said. He was beyond giving excuses or caring what she thought. He wanted the man's name and anything else she could tell him. "Do you want a drink?"

"Better not. I'm not really supposed to be in here."

"Oh. Sorry." He glanced round them. "I don't want to get you into trouble."

"You won't."

"Did you get a chance to talk to your friend on reception?"

"Yes."

She was making the most of it, enjoying having him on the end of a line. And no doubt feeling it was no more than her due after the way he'd been keeping away from her.

"Did she know the man's name?"

"Yes." And finally: "It was a Mr. Donnachie. Adrian Donnachie."

It meant nothing to Martyn. "Adrian Donnachie," he repeated, and wondered what more he could ask.

"He registered a London address," she said. "I can get it for you if you like."

"No. No, it's all right, thanks." He could always ask her later if need be.

"And he was here for just the one night. Arrived in the afternoon and left the following morning."

"Right."

"Anyway, look, I'll have to go. Why don't you come up on one of my nights off?"

He made a vague promise, the least he could do in return for her work on his behalf. She scuttled off back to the restaurant.

Coming out of the hotel, he saw for the first time the view that had given it its name. There was a three-quarter moon illuminating the black lagoon of Coniston Water snaking away between towering hills.

Adrian Donnachie. It meant nothing but gave him a trump card to put before Julie should he ever need it. Was it being foolishly optimistic to hope that Mr. Donnachie's visit might have been his last? That, having collected his two grand, he'd gone back to London well satisfied and with no thought of returning?

There was a sense in which Martyn hoped not. In London he would remain an unreachable and continuing threat. At least if he came back for more there'd be the possibility of confrontation and of settling things once and for all.

XV

He breakfasted alone the following morning and read *The Times,*
which he'd picked up on his way back from his run. There was
fighting in Lebanon, and talks over the future of Hong Kong were
going badly. At ten o'clock he heard Julie shuffling about between her bedroom and the bathroom. Then she appeared in the
kitchen looking hung over and drawn.

"Hi," she said.

"Hi. Sleep all right?"

"Yes."

He poured her some coffee while she lit herself a cigarette. She
was without makeup and had her hair tucked back behind her
ears. It made her look younger and more vulnerable.

"Sorry about last night," she said with a yawn.

"My fault."

"No, it wasn't."

He took the coffee to her and she put up her face for a kiss. So
they were friends again. Well, that much was a relief. She made a
vicious opponent and he'd settle for having her on his side any-
time. Though he wondered what the terms of their armistice
would turn out to be and whether he'd be able to abide by them.

"I've been thinking," she said. "About you."

"Oh yes?"

"About how it must be for you living here. With only me for
company—and that's when I'm not either stoned out of my head
or screaming blue murder at you. It can't be much fun."

"If you want me to go . . ." he began.

"I don't!" She spoke with such vehemence that she had to close
her eyes a moment as her hangover asserted itself. "I don't want
you to go," she said more quietly. "If I did then I'd say so. I just
don't want you feeling trapped, that's all. I don't want you to feel
any sort of . . . obligation."

He nodded, grateful for what she was saying but aware at the same time that it was all now a bit beside the point. The ties that bound them weren't just those of affection and an unwillingness to hurt one another; they were to do with the body in the copse and the shadowy Mr. Donnachie who'd travelled up from London to collect his two grand. Until all that was sorted there could be no question of his going anywhere.

She extended the hand that wasn't holding the cigarette and began to play with the hairs on his arm. "What about a job?"

"A job?" he echoed.

"When I first met you, you used to talk about becoming a philosopher."

"I did what?"

"Oh yes, it's no use denying it. You were going to become one of this country's top philosophers. You were going to open a boutique or a circus or whatever it is that philosophers have."

He'd seen her come to life like this before. No matter how bad the hangover, the first few sips of coffee and drags on her cigarette would dispel it and she'd be back on form.

"I don't want to be a philosopher anymore."

"No? What put you off the idea?"

"Socrates."

"Why? What's he been saying?"

"It's not what he's been saying. It's what happened to him."

"And what was that?"

"He was forced to take poison."

It was an idea that intrigued her. "Really?"

"Yes. Hemlock. He was found guilty of corrupting the country's youth."

"Which country?"

"Greece."

"I've been there. I wonder if I saw him."

"I doubt it. This was Ancient Greece."

"Well, it's quite a while since I went."

They decided to go out for a walk, ignoring the distant, dark clouds that threatened rain. For a change they would head into the forest and away from the lake shore. Julie excused herself and went to put on a sweater and some shoes while Martyn tidied away the breakfast things.

He'd already done some careful thinking about the mysterious Mr. Donnachie while out on his run. There was something decidedly odd about a blackmailer who took his victim out to dinner at the town's poshest hotel. Odder still that he should then stay the night before leaving at his leisure the following day. Blackmailers traditionally remained anonymous and communicated either by phone—with a handkerchief over the mouthpiece—or by grotesque letters made up of bits cut from newspapers. They demanded the money be left in wastepaper baskets or left-luggage lockers. What they didn't do was make appointments for dinner.

"Ready then?" sang out Julie as she came back in wearing woollies and a bobble cap.

"Yes, OK," he said. "Nature lesson time is it?"

"Oh, sure. The only nature I know about's the birds and bees. And then it's a kinky version."

It'd become a joke between them, her ignorance of the countryside around. Martyn, who was no naturalist himself, had pointed out the different flowers and shrubs in the garden, and the weeds growing between them.

"Very nice," she said. "Only can't we just buy some chemicals to put on that'll sort it all out for us?"

There was a path between the trees for them to follow, though it was little used and disappeared altogether in places, to reappear as a faint impression some twenty or thirty yards further on. They walked hand in hand, having to change to single file where the trees crowded in on them. The ground was everywhere thick with pine needles. Martyn pointed out the blue juniper berries that were beginning to show and, further on, the clumps of red that were the berries of the rowan ash.

"Are they edible?" asked Julie, showing a polite interest.

"The birds might think so but I don't think you would."

They trudged along for almost an hour, climbing all the time until they reached the crest of the crag. Wherever the natural growth of the forest had been thinned or cut down, it'd been supplemented by plantation so that their walk took them through areas where birch, pine and ash came randomly and at various heights and then through other areas where man's hand showed itself in the uniform rows of pines.

"Can we stop for a rest please?" pleaded Julie.

"Yes, sorry. Any time you like."

They found the stump of a chestnut tree to perch on. Julie settled down contentedly and lit a cigarette. Martyn, more restless, stayed beside her for a minute or two then wandered away to explore the surrounding forest.

There were only two reasons he could think of for Donnachie to have scorned the customary anonymity of the blackmailer and met Julie in the public setting of the Lake View Hotel. Either would also explain how he'd come to know about the killing.

Either, he'd previously known Senior, or he'd previously known Julie. Perhaps he'd worked with one or the other of them; perhaps they'd been part of the same "firm."

Take hypothesis number one. That Donnachie was a friend or colleague of the dead man. What happens? He knows where his friend is going and why. However, the friend disappears without trace. Donnachie thinks about it, then rings Julie. Tells her she'd better meet him or else. Or else what? says Julie. Or else he'll take what he knows, not to the police, but the gangland bosses who sent Senior on his mission and would lose no time in sending someone else to avenge him. Julie has no choice. OK, she says, eight o'clock at the Lake View Hotel, dress informal.

"Isn't this lovely?" she called from her seat on the tree trunk.

"What?" he said, his mind elsewhere.

"Well, all this. Being up here. It's beautiful."

Nevertheless, when she'd finished her cigarette and they were ready to move again, he couldn't persuade her to follow the path any further to where it led over the summit of the crag.

"Haven't we come far enough?" she argued. "I think we should set off back."

"I thought you were enjoying it."

"I am. So let's quit while we're ahead."

He let her have her way and they set off downhill, retracing their steps. As they did so, he noticed a particularly large pine cone which he picked off the forest floor and gave to her.

"Here. Help you tell what the weather's going to do."

"You mean it's got a little radio inside it?"

"I mean if it opens then it's going to be fine. If it closes then it's going to rain."

They came to the point where the track was at its steepest and had to concentrate on their feet. The hard brown pine needles were as treacherous as ice.

Hypothesis number two. That Julie had known Donnachie as a friend in London. Perhaps she'd told him herself about the killing, expecting sympathy, but finding only that there was no honour among villains and that Donnachie demands a price for keeping his mouth shut. She arranges the meeting at the hotel, hoping she can talk him out of it. While at the same time taking the money along in case she can't. Then comes back without the money. Ergo: she hasn't been able to talk him out of it.

They arrived back at the bungalow to find they'd left the front door unlocked. To be on the safe side, Martyn went in first and checked through the rooms.

"It's all right," he called. "No intruders."

"Of course there aren't," she said, following him in. "Nobody to intrude, is there." She placed the pine cone on the kitchen table.

He reheated the coffee and poured cups for both of them.

"Cheers," she said. "And listen, I was serious about what I was saying earlier."

"About what?"

"About you leaving here and getting a job. And, all right, perhaps not as a philosopher. But as something else instead."

"I suppose it's time I was thinking about it, yes," he said carefully.

She saw his misgivings but misunderstood the reason for them. "Oh, it's not that I want you to go or that I want to get rid of you. You don't really think that, do you?"

"No."

"Honestly?"

She came to him and they embraced. It surprised him to find how close they were again, as though they'd fallen back in love. Perhaps their row of last night had been long overdue, a much needed clearing of the air.

"And if you did leave," she said, still in his arms, "you could always come back."

"Promise?"

"Only if you'll promise that you will come back. That you won't forget about me altogether."

"OK," he said, "it's a deal."

And they shook hands solemnly before embracing again.

"Coffee's going cold," she murmured and moved away from him. They sat down, facing across the table.

"Suppose I did get a job and had to leave," he said, "what would you do?"

"I'd probably cry. Then get drunk. Then . . . then I don't know."

"You'd stay here?"

"To start with, yes."

"But in the long term?"

"I've never had any long terms."

"You mean you don't know what you'd do."

"Not a clue. I mean I ended up here because I'd decided to make a break from the London scene. And I'd been staying here for odd times anyway."

"While your friend was in the hospital."

"Yes. So when I wanted to get the hell out of London this was the obvious place to come to. But I don't think I ever saw it as being forever."

"Might you go back to London?"

She hesitated. "I suppose I might, yes."

"And do what?"

She slowly shook her head. "Not what I was doing before. Otherwise I don't know." Then, with a gesture of helplessness: "I mean perhaps you should leave. For my sake. Perhaps it's the only way I'll ever get my act together and decide what the hell it is I want to do." Then she glanced up at the window and said, "Hey, look."

"What?"

"It's starting to rain."

There were spots hitting the glass and then running swiftly down it. She picked up the pine cone, which had remained open.

"And look at this. The darn thing's not working."

"Must be faulty."

"Can't we send it back?"

She went and placed it on the windowsill and among a cluster of small plant pots, among whose neglected inhabitants only the cactus plants were surviving. Then she sat down again and lit a cigarette.

He decided to risk their rediscovered affection and harmony by asking the one question that mattered. The one they were conveniently ignoring with all this talk of his leaving and what she might do subsequently.

"So what about the money you took?" he said quietly.

She gave a groan of dismay but he saw immediately it was going to be all right: this time she wasn't going to fly off the handle. Keeping it light, she said, "I thought you'd forgotten about that."

"I wish I could. I really do."

"Then try harder."

He was gently insistent. "It wasn't an old school friend of yours, was it? Please, Julie, tell me the truth. Otherwise don't talk to me about leaving. Don't talk to me about doing anything, because this business of the money is going to get in the way all the time."

"All right," she said flatly, "there was no school friend. Sorry. I'll do a hundred lines, shall I—I must not tell lies."

"You gave that money to somebody though?"

"I suppose I must have, mustn't I?"

"Who?"

She slowly shook her head: she wasn't going to tell him that. Since he knew it anyway, Martyn let it go.

"All right then, answer me this—was he blackmailing you?"

She looked at him, opened her mouth to speak, then closed it again. She looked round as though seeking an ally, or a distraction, or anyway some tactic by which she could avoid answering the question. Until, finding none of these things, she had to answer and did so quietly: "No."

"I don't believe you."

"So why ask?"

"Julie, if somebody is blackmailing you, then it's serious. It puts us—and I say us, not just you but both of us—in one hell of a fix. We can't go to the police. We can't go to anybody. So. Please tell me the truth."

"Will you believe me if I do?"

"Try me."

"All I can say, Martyn, is that there's nothing for you to worry about. Nothing. And, as you said before, it's my money and I can drop it down the loo or feed it to the birds if I want to. All you need worry about is whether it's going to involve you."

He interrupted quickly. "Believe it or not, I do worry about you as well."

"Yes, OK," she relented, "I know you do. All I'm saying is—I don't have to tell you what I did with the money or who I gave it to, just so long as I can tell you—which I do—cross my heart, scouts' honour and all that—there's no problem, no aggro, no danger. And there's definitely—and I do mean definitely with a capital everything—definitely no chance of anybody finding out about the body."

He sat and looked at her. "You mean because you've paid him off?"

"Please, Martyn. I've told you all I'm going to tell you."

"Don't they always say you can never pay off a blackmailer? That they always come back?"

"Do they."

"Yes, they do. So how do you know he's not going to come back?"

But she pursed her lips and shook her head: she'd said her piece and wasn't going to add to it.

"Well then, just tell me one thing," he said.

She still didn't answer.

"Just one thing," he urged.

"What?"

"Does the person you gave the money to know about the killing?"

"If I answer will that be an end to this? Is that really all you want to know?"

"Yes." He wanted more of course, much more, but would settle for what he could get. "Yes, that's all I want to know."

"Well then, yes. He does."

He'd expected her to say no.

"He does? He knows about the knife and everything and the way we buried the body?"

"Yes."

"Jesus," he said. "Oh Christ."

He realised suddenly how all along he'd been hoping to be

proved wrong. Had been expecting that sooner or later she'd come up with a blushing explanation of how the money had gone to pay a gambling debt or for new clothes or jewellery—anything but to have his worst fears confirmed.

"But you've got to believe me, Martyn," she urged, "there's nothing for you to worry about."

"Oh no?"

"No!" She was becoming angry and insistent. "Now please, Martyn, you've asked me to and so I've told you the truth. And I'm also telling you the truth when I say there's no danger."

"But he knows? This man knows?"

She ignored his questions. "Do you believe me when I say there's no danger?"

"How can there be no danger if he knows?"

She was near to shouting. "Because I've dealt with him! I've talked to him. It's all right!"

He shook his head. How could it be? How could anything be all right again?

"Do you believe me or not?"

"It's not a matter of whether I believe you . . ."

"Yes, it is," she insisted. "For me it is. Do you?"

He shrugged. "I believe that's what you think."

"That's what I know. I know because I've spoken to this man. And there's nothing to fear from him. So if you want to leave here —if you want to go and get a job—then don't let that stop you. Now—do you believe me or not?"

Whatever he said, it wouldn't alter the situation. He mustered as much conviction as he could.

"I believe you, yes."

She nodded, apparently satisfied. The rain was now drumming steadily against the window and on the sill the pine cone had finally closed.

XVI

Neither of them mentioned the money again. It wasn't that he was happy with the situation. On the contrary, he couldn't believe that the two thousand quid had been the end of it and lived each day in fear of what might be to come. But he sensed Julie would resent any further questions. And he'd no wish to antagonise her. They'd enemies enough without throwing punches at one another.

Taking her at her word, he applied for a couple of jobs—one with the BBC and another with a London publishing house.

"When do you expect to hear from them?" she asked, seeing him writing his letters of application.

"Never."

"Then why're you applying?"

"Force of habit. And because you told me to."

"Don't you have any contacts? Anybody who could help you?"

"No."

Except for her, he thought. She could probably pull a few strings and land him a job subediting pornographic magazines.

It was beginning to go dark by five in the evening. The oil-fired central heating was switched on and turned to high. There was something of the hibernating animal about Julie, who liked to keep warm and insisted on stocking up for the coming winter. They returned from the supermarket with the car boot packed with cigarettes, frozen food, whisky and dried milk.

Perhaps, after all, winter would be the worst they'd have to face. Other things—such as ignominy and imprisonment—might yet pass them by.

"I don't fancy going out tonight," said Julie. It was just a week since she'd kept her appointment with Donnachie. "How about a takeaway?"

He went into town on his bike and returned with portions of

sweet-and-sour pork, fried rice, prawn crackers, spareribs and egg foo yung inside foil containers. They sat in the kitchen to eat.

"You know the hospital," she said suddenly.

"The one that . . ." He wasn't sure how to identify it.

"The Holy Rosary. Where you followed me."

"Yes."

"I got a letter from them. About how desperate they are for money. Not that that's anything new. They're always desperate for money."

"But don't they charge people?" he asked between mouthfuls of fried rice. "It's a private hospital isn't it?"

"Yes. They should be making a bomb but, being nuns, they don't want to. They charge the absolute minimum. Which is why they're always flat broke."

Martyn grunted sympathetically, not sure where all this was leading. Julie said nothing more until they'd finished eating and had gone into the lounge to watch the late news on TV.

"They're a lot more worldly than you think, you know," she said, lighting a cigarette. "Nuns."

"Yes?"

"I don't mean they're not holy and all that. Just that nothing shocks or frightens them. I mean they've all kinds of weirdos to deal with in there. And then, like I say, they're permanently on the edge of bankruptcy. But it doesn't worry them in the least."

"Must be having God on their side," offered Martyn.

"Must be. Though you'd think He might help them a bit more than He does."

"You've never been tempted to join?" he asked jovially. "Take the veil or whatever they call it?"

She smiled. "I don't think I'd get in. Don't you have to be a virgin?"

It was only later, when the news was over and they were watching an old John Wayne film, that she finally reached what sounded like the real point and purpose of this talk about hospitals and nuns.

"They've asked me to be on a committee."

"Who have?"

"The sisters."

"Ah." He'd been slow to realise they were back on the topic again.

"They're trying to raise money for a new ward. I mean as well as keep the usual wolf from the door. So there's going to be a committee, and they've asked me to be on it."

He observed her. "I'd never thought of you as a committee person."

"Neither have I. But you try saying no to a nun. It's not easy."

He had the strange yet distinct impression he was watching a performance. One in which he didn't believe for a minute.

"How many are on this committee?"

"What?"

He repeated his question.

"Oh, I don't know. Probably me, Sister Veronica and a gang of dried-out alkies and born-again heroin addicts."

It was all pat and bright and delivered with a studied casualness that might have fooled him three months ago but not now.

"When did they ask you?"

"Oh . . . just today."

"You went to the hospital today?"

"They rang me here. They may be nuns and unworldly and all that but telephones they can manage."

He let the matter drop, though he'd have sworn there wasn't a word of truth in anything she'd said. Except that, all right, the nuns may well have been short of money—nuns usually were. But the rest—the new ward and the committee which Julie (of all people) had been invited to join—all had a sickeningly hollow ring to it.

Perhaps he could have tripped her up with further questions but it might not have been wise. Better he should wait and see what her game was before deciding on his own next move.

The following afternoon he went into town in search of new reading matter, picked up two paperback thrillers at half price and returned to the bungalow as Julie was brewing a pot of tea.

"Oh, I heard from the hospital," she said without looking at him. "They rang while you were out."

"Oh yes?"

"There's going to be a meeting of that committee I told you about."

"When?"

"Tomorrow night. Half-seven."

She was going to meet Adrian Donnachie. He was convinced of it. She was going to meet him and hand over a further instalment in the price of silence.

Yet he couldn't challenge her and call her a liar for fear she might admit it. What would he say then? That she shouldn't go? That she should refuse to hand over another penny and defy Donnachie to do his worst? He doubted he had the nerve for that.

"I can't say I'm looking forward to it," she chatted on. "In fact I wish I'd made an excuse. Said I was ill. But that's another thing about nuns. They're bloody difficult to lie to."

Besides, she was doing all this for his sake as much as her own. Indeed, perhaps it was his involvement that made her vulnerable. Where she might have once cheerfully arranged to have the blackmailing Mr. Donnachie bumped off (or whatever), the risk of incriminating Martyn now prevented her. Hence this tissue of lies, under cover of which she could slip out to a sordid and perhaps dangerous rendezvous with their blackmailer. The least he could do was play along.

"You might surprise yourself and enjoy the meeting."

"I doubt it. But I might be late back. I've no idea how long these things go on for."

She left at seven-fifteen, calculating aloud for his benefit that she'd be ten minutes late in arriving but then she supposed committees were a bit late like parties and it wouldn't do to be there on the dot.

"How do I look?"

"Delicious."

She was wearing calfskin boots, bottle-green khaki trousers and a loose-knit jumper with fringed shoulder pads.

"You don't think anyone'll mistake me for a nun?"

"They deserve to be in that hospital if they do."

She gave him a quick kiss on the forehead, then left. He listened to her driving away, relieved to know the deception was over even if something more serious might be about to begin.

As far as he was aware, she hadn't been near the kitchen drawer with its wads of notes. He hadn't expected her to. After all the trouble to concoct the hospital story, she was unlikely to repeat her mistake of last time and let him see just how much cash had gone. All the same, he went to look, knowing that even the best-laid schemes could fall prey to the silliest of cockups.

There was about the same amount of money in the drawer as yesterday. Certainly no large amount had been taken. If he were right and she had gone to pay off Donnachie, then the money was coming from elsewhere.

He went into her bedroom and began to search her untidy dressing table with its crammed drawers. He remembered—or thought he did—seeing her once take her chequebook from one of them. He found it in the top left-hand drawer, amid a small tip of makeup, screwed-up bills and soiled tissues.

The violation of her privacy caused him few qualms. What else could he do? At stake was the freedom and safety of them both. And, anyway, such niceties of conscience proved to be beside the point as he opened her chequebook, riffled through its stubs, and found that not one of them was filled in. There were no dates, no amounts, no anything. He replaced it in the drawer, allowing himself a wry smile. Typical that her carelessness should so effectively guard her secrets from prying eyes.

Though what was he really after anyway with all this searching through drawers? Did he really need more evidence than he had already? She'd lied to him about the two thousand pounds—the "old school friend" story—then admitted it'd gone to Donnachie and that he knew all about the disposal of the body. On top of which had come these new lies, designed to camouflage a second meeting with their blackmailer.

He buckled on his leathers, went outside and mounted his bike. He knew where he was going but little else. He'd no plan, no strategy . . . just an irresistible feeling that he couldn't again remain sitting it out on the bench while Julie went in to bat for both of them.

It took him less than ten minutes to reach the Lake View Hotel with its large floodlit car park. Being mid-week and out of season, there were few cars in evidence. The Porsche wasn't among them.

Martyn hesitated but then parked his bike and dismounted.

The absence of the Porsche suggested they'd chosen elsewhere for their appointment. Nevertheless he was on his guard as he went up the steps and into the foyer of the hotel.

Even so, he was spotted. Seen by someone who was coming out of the lift as he was scrutinising the near-deserted receptions and the bar beyond.

"Martyn, hi. You looking for me?"

It was Wendy Harriman, out of uniform and in a fawn duffle coat, apparently on her way out. As always, she seemed pleased to see him.

"I thought you might be here," he said evasively.

"Well, I am. Off-duty as well. Let me buy you a drink."

"Don't let me keep you if you're going somewhere."

"You're not," she said quickly. "We can go in here if you like." —the hotel bar—"They don't mind staff using it when we're as quiet as this."

They took their drinks to a table in the corner from where he could keep an eye on the main door. He needed to bring the conversation round to the mysterious Mr. Donnachie but without admitting it was in search of him—and not her—that he'd come to the hotel.

"When was it I last saw you?" he said with the air of one thinking aloud. "When we went to the Crown, wasn't it?"

"Yes."

"You were telling me about Julie's dining companion. The guy from London. Donnachie or whatever his name was."

"Wasn't I just," she said.

There was a pause while he waited for more. When it wasn't forthcoming he thought, that's it then, he's not here after all.

But she was playing her own game, too, and let a full five seconds pass before saying, "He's here again."

Martyn gave a start he was unable to disguise. Wendy was watching him.

"Didn't you know?"

"No." It was at least as true as yes would have been.

"Well, he is. Came this afternoon."

It gave him no comfort to know he'd been right all along. Rather it was confirmation things were every bit as bad as he'd feared.

Still he could do nothing about it, not knowing where they'd gone, and so remained with Wendy, steering the conversation onto easier topics. How long was she planning to stay on at the hotel? Had she had any auditions lately?

"There's this fringe group I might get some work with in London. I know the director."

"Good," he said, pleased for her.

"What about you?"

He shrugged. "Can't stay here forever I suppose but . . . haven't got much in the way of alternatives just now." And he told her about the two jobs he'd applied for.

They finished their drinks and ordered more. She seemed to have permanently cancelled her night out, wherever it was, while he had no option but to sit it out and wait for Donnachie to return.

"Tell me about your lady friend," she challenged him.

"Not a lot to tell," he said carefully. "She used to be a model in London and she's come up here for a break."

"How old is she?"

"Would you believe me if I said I didn't know?"

"I bet she's thirty-five."

Martyn smiled and shook his head: he wasn't going to help her with her guessing. Though he couldn't blame her for trying. They must have caused a fair amount of speculation over the summer: the tall well-spoken young man and the golden-haired older woman. How much more they might yet cause didn't bear thinking about.

Fortunately Wendy seemed to lose interest and went on to entertain him with stories of life at the hotel, which sounded pretty much the same as life everywhere and were mainly to do with thieving and sex. Peccadillos compared to Martyn's own immediate past but entertaining enough to keep them there talking and drinking for another hour before she asked unexpectedly, "Do you want to see my room?"

It was the kind of tricky situation—preliminary to seduction by ex-lover while on the lookout for return of blackmailer of present lover—for which Martyn needed his wits about him. But his wits had gone, scattered by the beer he'd been steadily putting away. Even his months with Julie hadn't given him a better head.

"Why not?" he said and smiled vaguely.

"It's grotty," she warned him, "but at least it is mine. Some of the other girls have to share."

He gave a slight lurch as he stood. How much had they had to drink? First he'd bought a round, then she had, then he'd bought another . . .

"Come on," she said, and led him to the lift. "It's the top floor, as if you couldn't guess."

And what time was it? He managed to catch a glimpse of a clock before the lift doors slid closed. Nearly ten. There was no telling what time Julie would return, or even if she'd come back to the hotel at all. Only Donnachie had to come back there. And if he did so alone Martyn would have no way of recognising him.

Wendy nuzzled up to him in the lift. "I've never forgotten, you know, when we were together."

"Neither have I," he said, and kissed her.

The room was every bit as small as she'd warned him so that they went in through the door and all but fell onto the bed.

"I've got some vodka," she said, reaching down to the beside cabinet.

" 'S all right," he said. "Don't drink vodka."

"I'm not sure what else we have to offer."

He began to explain he wasn't really thirsty at all before recognising the suggestive response for what it was. He gave a small, belated laugh.

He'd ended up lying on the bed, which was so small that his feet stuck out over the end. Wendy was perched on the edge like a sickroom visitor. It was oppressively hot and the feather pillow cradled his neck. Another two minutes and he'd be asleep. He sat up and pulled off his jacket.

Taking this as her cue, Wendy peeled off her sweater. "I'll race you," she said.

She won easily and sat there nude watching him as he undid the buttons of his shirt.

"You've done this before," he joked.

"And so have you," she said. "So get a bloody move on."

They pushed the clothes onto the floor so she could snuggle down beside him on the bed. Her body was familiar territory despite the months since they'd been together. He knew her movements and responded effortlessly, surprised to be reminded of how well they made love together.

He lay, spent, on the bed, telling himself he mustn't go to sleep. She was up against him, an arm over his shoulder and a leg hooked over his thigh.

"Are you going to stay with that woman?" she asked, her voice muffled by the bedclothes.

He didn't reply. Their lovemaking might have given her the right to ask but he didn't want to betray Julie with his answer.

"Why don't you come back to London with me?" she said, trying again.

Why didn't he? Well, because of Julie of course. And because of the threat Adrian Donnachie held over them both. Donnachie whom she was seeing that night and who might already be back in the hotel. All his fears came seeping back.

"I don't know what I'm going to do," he said, springing off the bed and sorting out his clothes from among those on the floor.

"Will you tell me when you do?"

He hesitated a moment, then said, "Yes."

"Promise."

"I promise."

She pulled the bedclothes around her and lay watching him get dressed.

"Do you mind if I stay here? Only I'm on early tomorrow."

"No." He'd rather she did. Once downstairs, he'd have to be on his guard. "I'll find my way out. And you look after yourself." He leaned over to kiss her goodbye.

"Promise you'll tell me when you've decided what you're going to do," she said sleepily.

"I promise. See you."

He went out into the corridor. Where the lights were on time switches and had gone out so that he had to fumble his way along in near darkness. Then he found he'd set off in the wrong direction and had to retrace his steps, though at least he did find a switch which made things easier. The lift was engaged so he went down the stairs alongside it, finding them better lit and carpeted the further he descended.

The foyer was deserted. The receptionist gave him a cursory

glance from behind her desk: she'd seen him going up with Wendy.

Martyn wondered about asking—had Mr. Donnachie returned, please? Then wondered further what he'd say if the answer were yes. Perhaps such a direct approach should be kept for a last resort. He went out of the hotel into the car park.

The cold air made his head swim. He still hadn't got over the effects of the alcohol despite the session with Wendy in the hot little room. He walked to his bike. Should he go back to the bungalow or cruise around in the hope of bumping into Julie and friend?

He was still trying to decide when he heard the familiar Porsche engine approaching and ducked down lest the headlights should catch him. Julie's car appeared, ignored the open spaces of the car park and made for the front steps of the hotel. The engine remained idling and the headlights blazing while a man got out of the passenger side, said something, then slammed the door closed. The car was moving again even before he'd started up the steps. Its headlights sliced across the car park and then it was accelerating away and Martyn could straighten up, knowing he hadn't been spotted.

The receptionist looked up at him as he entered, this time giving a puzzled half smile. He nodded back, leaving her to make what she would of his comings and goings.

Donnachie was alone at the bar. He was younger than Martyn had expected, dark haired, stockily built and wearing a dark suit stylishly cut.

His voice carried to Martyn, cockney and assertive. "So where's the action in this place?"

The barman shrugged apologetically. "Not here anyway."

At the entrance to the bar was a pay phone, shrouded by its acoustic hood. Martyn stopped at it, dialled an incomplete number and stood holding the receiver. It was cover for a minute or two while he decided on his next step.

He was aware of Donnachie looking at him but it seemed a purposeless gaze. Then he was speaking again, his voice loud in the empty bar.

"See what I can find elsewhere then."

"Goodnight sir," intoned the barman.

Donnachie came past Martyn, heading for the door. Martyn heard him go out, waited as long as he dared, then put down the receiver and turned to follow.

"Just wanted to use the phone," he said to the receptionist.

"That's all right," she called cheerily.

Once outside, he found Donnachie to be some thirty or forty yards away, hands thrust into trouser pockets and striding away into the narrow streets of the town.

Martyn went to his bike and pulled on his helmet. Then he sat astride the machine and heaved it forward, pushing with his feet against the tarmac. It was heavy work on the flat, then he reached the beginnings of the slope and he was able to sit and let the bike, silent and without lights, carry him downwards in cautious pursuit.

XVII

Donnachie seemed to be making for the Grapes, a lakeside pub
that squatted almost on the shore itself where the road from town
dipped for a few hundred yards and stuck to the water's edge
before climbing away back into the trees.

It was the sort of pub—white-painted and festooned with lines
of coloured lights—designed to catch the eye and it seemed to
have caught Donnachie's. Martyn followed him in slow and silent
pursuit, freewheeling through the near-deserted streets of the
town. It wasn't until the final half mile that the descent exhausted
itself and the road buckled to follow the uneven lakeside con-
tours. By then Martyn was sure of Donnachie's destination and
was able to stop and wait, giving him time to reach the Grapes,
before firing the engine of the bike and letting it do the work of
carrying him there. At one point the narrow road was half-
blocked by roadworks—someone had dug a hole and decorated it
with tape—so that Martyn was glad he was now on full beam.

Despite the coloured lights and their promise of raucous company, the pub was quiet. It relied on tourists for summertime
prosperity, then ticked over on a sparse local trade through the
winter. Donnachie was at the bar ordering a large scotch and
soda; a group of youths were playing on the dartboard; there
might have been half-a-dozen other customers.

"A pint of bitter," said Martyn, then remembered too late how
much he'd drunk already. Never mind, he could leave most of the
beer if necessary.

Donnachie wore a faintly derisive smile as he gazed around
him, a visitor unimpressed by the primitive local culture. He
walked to the jukebox and studied the tunes on offer.

The bar formed three sides of a square so that Martyn was able
to move round to the side away from Donnachie and remain
largely hidden from him. He sipped at the beer and tried to focus

his thoughts on the fix he was in: all right, he'd successfully followed Donnachie this far—and no doubt could successfully follow him back to the Lake View Hotel or wherever he might go next—but what was the point of it all? What would he do at the end of it?

There was a sudden blast of music. Donnachie had invested in the jukebox. He'd also attracted the attention of the locals by the dartboard, one or two of whom were eyeing him with an undisguised curiosity. To judge from their expressions, they were as unimpressed by him as he'd been by them.

It struck Martyn that the simplest course of action would be to approach Donnachie and speak to him. Perhaps announce who he was and reveal he was in league with Julie. It would show she wasn't alone but had an ally. He could even try threatening Donnachie. Hint that whatever he'd been paid tonight was the final—very final—instalment; if he came back for more he'd regret it.

Could he really carry it off though? Put on a convincing performance as a leather-jacketed heavy? He feared that he'd turn out neither enough of a thug nor enough of an actor.

He'd drunk half the beer. Careful, he thought. Got to keep a clear head. And something else too. He needed to visit the gents, which meant passing the group at the dartboard and coming into Donnachie's field of vision. He'd have to risk it.

"Looks a wanker to me," said one of the dart-throwing gang as Martyn sidled past.

They were talking about Donnachie then. And in voices loud enough for him to hear. At the moment he didn't seem to be taking much notice but was staring idly at the collection of framed prints behind the bar.

Martyn peed up against the cracked porcelain and wondered if there was going to be trouble and where it would leave him if there were. The thought flitted through his mind—how convenient if Donnachie were to meet an untimely end at the hands of local yobboes and thus be neatly disposed of without Martyn having to lift a finger. Wishful and unpleasant thinking.

He came out through the double doors of the gents and saw that little had changed: the yobboes were still chucking darts in the direction of the board and barbed comments in the direction of Donnachie—though now Donnachie was no longer affecting not to hear but was returning their hard stares. At the same time the music came to an end, leaving the bar in a prickly silence. Martyn felt anything might happen and would probably do so within the next five minutes.

"Hey, Johnny," called out the man behind the bar. He had the air of being the landlord, a man on his own territory. He was also big, unshaven and overweight.

"What?" said one of the youths at the dartboard.

"Here," said the landlord, and jerked his head to show he wanted Johnny up at the bar where he could speak to him.

Johnny muttered rebelliously, though inaudibly, and wandered over.

"Yeah?"

The landlord leant over the bar and spoke quietly, too quietly for Martyn to hear, but he could guess at the gist of what was said. From the way Johnny glanced resentfully at Donnachie before slouching back to his mates and passing on a muttered message it seemed clear they were being warned off causing any aggro. Evidently the Grapes was a respectable house, one that didn't expect its passing trade to be done over by the regulars.

Martyn wondered what it was about Donnachie that had seemed to antagonise so quickly. Was it just his manner, or the way he'd commandeered the jukebox without so much as a by your leave, or did he carry with him the faint aroma of menace brought from another, murkier world?

Whatever it was, the landlord's instructions to cool it seemed to have done the trick. Donnachie was left in peace to drink his second scotch and soda. The darters played on. Martyn sipped at his beer, not sure whether to be sorry or relieved there'd been no trouble.

"Goodnight," said Donnachie from the other side of the bar.

It was a gesture less of politeness than of provocation. I come and go when I like, it announced, and sod the lot of you. A couple of the dart players eyed him as he departed.

Martyn left what remained of his pint and went after him. He did so in an unhurried fashion, saying his own goodnight to the landlord and sneaking a look at the locals who were showing no interest in his departure. Outside it was now set for a cold, clear night, with enough moonlight to show Donnachie, hunched slightly against the cold, fifty yards away on the road to town.

Martyn couldn't take the bike, not if he were to stay behind Donnachie without being detected. He set out on foot, grateful for his rubber soles that were noiseless on the tarmac surface. Donnachie disappeared around the first bend. Martyn speeded up, taking longer strides. He'd have to be nearer than this for when they got into the tangled streets of the town.

It was his undoing. Donnachie, streetwise and well schooled in urban guerilla tactics, was waiting just round the bend, hidden among the shadows of the roadside trees. Martyn found a hand closing around his wrist. Caught off guard, he was flung sideways.

He heard himself cry out and was then jarred by the sudden contact with a tree trunk. He turned and was aware only of a wicked-looking blade that caught the moonlight and was pointed towards his jugular.

"What . . . ?" he gasped, his senses swimming. Then, beyond the blade, he saw Donnachie's face and felt a hand against his shoulder holding him against the tree.

"Just what's your fucking game then, eh?"

"What? No . . . nothing."

He was conscious only of Donnachie's intense stare and of the knife blade, which reminded him of Senior stretched out on the kitchen floor and the pool of blood.

"Seen you before, haven't I?"

"No. I mean . . . I don't know." Then, feeling that some kind of protest was called for, Martyn forced a note of self-righteousness into his voice. "Look, what the hell is this?"

"That's what I want to know."

"Are you after money or what?" asked Martyn, fear sharpening his wits and making him crafty.

"Fuck off," said Donnachie quietly. It meant he wasn't buying that: Martyn would have to try harder.

"I haven't got more than a few pounds . . ."

The knife silenced him, pricking the end of his chin.

"You were following me," said Donnachie. "Why?"

Martyn went to shake his head but the knife point held him like a mounted butterfly. "I wasn't, no," he said. "Just going home, that's all."

"Either you thought you could mug me," said Donnachie as if Martyn hadn't spoken. "Or you thought you could do a favour for your mates back there."

"I was going home," repeated Martyn. "I didn't even see you."

Donnachie studied him. He seemed unsure. It made Martyn wonder what he could say to swing the decision in his favour and get the dreadful knife removed.

"Open your jacket," said Donnachie finally.

Martyn pulled off his leather gauntlets then, fumblingly, took hold of the zip and pulled it. It took all his control to hold the jacket open, baring himself to the night air and the knife. Donnachie's free hand felt around his chest and under his arms.

"All right," he said, and Martyn at last knew that things were going his way.

"I was just going home," he repeated dully.

"If I see you again," said Donnachie, "then you'll be fucking dead." The knife blade came down from his chin and hovered around his chest. "You got that?"

Martyn said nothing. He knew he'd passed the test—somehow scraping through—and now had only to wait, let the other man have his say and the ordeal would be over. Though not without a souvenir. He winced as the knife nicked the back of his right hand and drew blood.

"Go on then," said Donnachie, nodding towards the road, "only you first this time."

Not needing to be told twice, Martyn edged round the smaller man, then started to walk briskly away. His hand smarted and he could feel the blood welling but couldn't yet take the time to stop and investigate. He risked a quick backwards glance and saw Donnachie beginning to follow.

He was trembling, physically upset by the encounter. Yet, strangely, he felt himself calmer, no longer irresolute, as though something had been settled between them. It wasn't an outcome —that had still to be decided—but at least weapons had now been chosen and he knew for the first time what he must do.

He walked faster, needing to get further ahead. Another backwards glance. Donnachie seemed to be walking in a regular pace, undismayed by Martyn's acceleration.

The road twisted, taking Martyn out of the sight of his adversary. It also brought him to the small cluster of roadworks he'd passed on his approach to the pub. It was marked off by a red-and-white tape and winking orange lights. The tape was anchored and held in place by steel poles, each about a yard long, driven into the ground and with a loop in the top to hold the tape. With barely a break in his stride, Martyn bent and wrenched one of them free, at the same time releasing it from the tape. Mercifully it came away first time and he was able to continue up the road, hugging it to him.

He slowed his pace, wanting Donnachie to see him and be reassured—before the next bend would carry him again out of his view. Once round it, he stepped off the roadway and into the bordering trees, flattening himself behind the first one that was wide enough to hide him and concentrating on controlling his breathing and slowing his beating heart.

The wait took an age, so long that he twice decided he'd been rumbled—Donnachie must be taking evading action and would any minute now appear behind him, knife held out and thrusting for Martyn's kidneys. Perhaps it was the roadworks that had given the game away: the way one corner of the tape now trailed unsupported. Perhaps anything.

Then suddenly Donnachie had appeared, walking with the steady plod of a man on his way to his bed, a man caught out by tiredness and too much drink. Martyn held his breath and tried to clear his mind of all but technical considerations: at what moment, and how, would it be best to strike? Donnachie approached, was masked by the tree that hid Martyn, then reappeared on the other side.

Martyn, holding his breath—and the metal bar—saw him reach the spot where he'd judged he must strike. If he were ever going to. Part of him had known all along he'd be unable to act when it came to it—he wasn't a murderer; it was as simple as that—so it amazed him now to find his feet really were carrying him forward and he was swinging the steel rod with all the force he could muster.

Too late, Martyn's footsteps warned Donnachie. He'd half-turned and was bringing up his left arm in a protective gesture when the blow caught him across the side of his neck. It was like the swatting of a baseball—but with the bat of steel and a ball of flesh and gristle. With a throttled "Ugh!" of surprise, Donnachie was flung sideways across the road into the shallow ditch at the other side.

It had to have killed him. If not then . . . well, that was that. Even while feeling the weight of the steel rod in his hands, Martyn knew he couldn't use it again. Not, anyway, on an inert, defenceless body.

There was no movement nor sound from Donnachie. Martyn grabbed a shoulder and pulled the body over. The face that gazed up at him was marked by the onset of surprise and fright but the eyes were lifeless and unseeing. He was dead all right. The way the head was twisted suggested the blow had snapped his neck. Here was a man who would never again operate flick knives, order scotch and sodas, or blackmail himself and Julie.

It was a moment of realisation and relief quickly overshadowed by the fear of more immediate dangers. Having killed Donnachie, he now had to get rid of him. And soon. The road wouldn't stay deserted forever.

As a precaution he rolled the body into deeper shadow where it would be invisible to passing cars. He had to think. First of all the steel rod, the murder weapon. He could send it javelinlike off into the trees or—better still—put it back where it'd come from. He listened hard but could hear no approaching traffic and so sprinted back to the roadworks, stuck the rod back into its hole and looped the tape over it.

Coming back, he realised what he must do with the body. For if it were ever found—at any time, anywhere—the tall motorcyclist seen hanging around the Lake View Hotel and then the Grapes about the time the deceased was known to have been in both places would be the first suspect.

The body had to vanish. Without leaving so much as a mark— or a ripple—to awaken suspicions.

For the second time in his life Martyn steeled himself, went down on one knee and lifted a dead body until it was balanced on one of his shoulders. This time, though, there wasn't any blood. Even the cut on his hand seemed to have dried up.

Bending slightly beneath his burden, he left the road and struck off across the field that he knew would bring him out onto the lake shore. Where he might meet anybody: midnight canoeists, courting couples, dog walkers . . . but he didn't believe he would. So much had gone his way already, it would have been churlish of fate to have thrown a spanner in the works at this late hour.

And, indeed, the narrow, stony beach was deserted. Now staggering under his load, he passed a familiar tree, then came to the dark mounds that crouched in a semicircle beyond the waterline. With a gasp of relief, he let Donnachie roll from off his shoulder.

There remained two minor obstacles, both of which he'd anticipated.

The boats, beached high and dry for the winter, were chained one to another. The two ends of the chain were then padlocked together; it was a lock to which Martyn no longer possessed a key. What he'd retained from his summer of boat minding though was an intimate knowledge of where one or two of the boats were rotting. He found the one he was looking for, took hold of the ring mounted on its bows and through which the chain passed and wrenched it loose.

The other problem was to find a suitable lump of wood to substitute for the oars Joe Hutton had stored away. He searched along the shore and finally came across a length of plank which, while far from ideal, was at least better than paddling with his empty hands.

Now there was the boat to be dragged to the water's edge, its keel screeching in protest. Then the body to be dragged down after it. As an afterthought he scouted around for some large stones and filled Donnachie's pockets. There was no current in the lake; once settled, the body should remain there forever.

He heaved it into the boat, threw in his piece of planking and then, with a well-practised technique, pushed off and jumped in.

It was hard work having to paddle the ungainly boat as though it were a canoe. He felt to be doing more waddling from side to side than going forward. Progress was slow. The planking was beginning to cut into his hands by the time he decided enough was enough. He still wasn't as far out from shore as he'd have ideally liked but then, the further he went, the further there'd be to go back. He allowed himself the luxury of a brief rest. There was no sense of depth to the water around him which was flat and black and still. Then, without looking at the face, he got his hands beneath Donnachie and half pushed, half lifted him over the side.

It was an effort that left the boat rocking wildly and forced Martyn to cling to one of the cross seats until it steadied again.

The body floated for a minute or two, slowly settling as the clothes took in water. Then there was a small gurgle and it'd gone, sliding away beneath the boat. Martyn thought of the time he'd made his desperate dive and saved the young girl. It couldn't have been too far from that spot where he was now dumping Donnachie.

He began the slow, awkward business of rowing back to shore. For a moment he was disoriented, failing to find the direction he wanted, but then the shoreline became familiar and he was able to aim for where the boats were parked in their semicircle. He reached the beach, jumped out and hauled his boat up to take its place again alongside its neighbours.

He could now walk. Regain his breath. Tell himself he'd no more to fear. If anyone asked, he'd had too much to drink and was clearing his head before trusting himself to riding his bike again. In truth, he felt giddy and light-headed though not from alcohol.

When he got to the Grapes, its coloured lights were all out and its car park empty but for Martyn's Suzuki parked where he'd left it. He got on and rode cautiously home.

As he'd expected, Julie was already there. The Porsche was evidence of that, as were the lights on in the house and the front door left unlocked.

"Is that you?" she sang out as he stumbled about in the hallway, pulling off his leathers and heavy boots.

"Yes."

"I'm having a bath."

Thank God, he thought. Conversation was the last thing he wanted.

They talked through the bathroom door.

"How was your meeting?" he asked.

"Oh, not too bad. Have you had a nice night?"

"Yeah. Only I'm tired. Going to bed."

"Oh, all right," she said, sounding a bit put out. "See you tomorrow then."

He climbed the steps to his attic room. He took off his clothes and lay on top of the bed, then, becoming cold, pulled the covers over him. He was exhausted and numb from the night's events yet felt as though he'd never be able to sleep again.

There was a sense—and he could now admit it—in which he must have intended to murder Donnachie all along. What other outcome had he imagined to his pursuit? That they'd have a chat and come to some sort of agreement? Never in a million years.

That he'd been capable of murder was less of a shock than he might have expected. To be honest, it'd been straightforward. Even easy. Tidying up afterwards had been physically arduous but, even then, he hadn't been racked by guilt. He'd been helped, of course, by the earlier killing of Senior in which he'd been an accomplice after the event. It had blunted his sensibilities and prepared him for the shock.

At least they were now free forever from the threat of blackmail. It'd been a messy, dreadful business but Donnachie could with some justice be said to have brought it on himself. His execution might have been legally indefensible but, viewed sympathetically, it was no more than the necessary removal of a pretty unpleasant character.

With these consoling thoughts to help him, Martyn finally dropped into a fitful sleep.

XVIII

The nightmares never came. He enjoyed a better night than he'd any right to expect and awoke the following morning with the mildest of hangovers.

The memory of last night's murder was instantly with him, but it didn't seem pressing. It'd happened and he'd now have to live with it but—Donnachie's point of view apart—it hadn't been the end of the world. In what had been a favourite phrase of his grandmother, it wasn't a hanging matter.

He came down from his attic room, drank a glass of water and went out for his early morning run.

He followed his regular route, which conveniently took him down to the lake edge and allowed him to check the body wasn't bobbing around on the water and hadn't been thrown up on the shore with the other flotsam. At least there was no wind to create currents that might do all end of mischief. It was a cold morning with a thin drizzle, a warning that winter was just around the corner. It'd be the real thing, too, up here in the Lakes, with enough ice and snow to leave scores of sheep and the odd human being dead of exposure.

There were no bodies to be seen yet though. Certainly not last night's. A few yards out floated a length of plank which Martyn recognised as his makeshift oar. As a sign from the lake whose significance he alone could understand, it was reassuring. Don't worry, it said, we've got the stiff and we'll make sure he stays put.

He wasn't worrying. Not, anyway, as he'd have thought he would.

There was something weird and unreal about his mood of carelessness. Was he then so hardened to violence as to take a murder in his stride? Perhaps living with Julie and her horror videos, to say nothing of the occasional corpse on the kitchen floor, had changed him more than he'd been aware. An even more chilling thought was that nature had fashioned him a cold, emotionless bastard from the word go. Hence his solitary path through life and the way women never stuck with him beyond a month or two. Or perhaps he was simply in a state of moral shock that would slowly wear off so that the guilt and remorse were yet to come.

In fact it was Julie who seemed to live the following days in a torpor of depression. It forced Martyn into a display of cheerful bonhomie in an attempt to raise her spirits and then, when that failed, into gently questioning her.

"Is anything the matter?"

She was instantly on the defensive. "What? No. Why should there be?"

He shook his head. "Just . . . you seem on edge."

"Perhaps it's because I'm sick of being cooped up in this bloody hole!"

And she stubbed out her cigarette, got to her feet and left the room.

It's all right, he wanted to reassure her. Donnachie's dead. There's nothing more to fear, no more money to be paid out, no more summonses to the Lake View Hotel to be answered. But of course he couldn't, and so had to watch each day as she went from being fidgety and ill at ease to being downright aggressive.

She reappeared in the doorway, with a jacket on and her hair pulled back under a headscarf.

"I'm going out." She spoke quietly, as if frightened of losing control.

"Do you want me to come?"

"No." Then, as an afterthought, "Thanks." And she went.

He knew better than to try to follow. Let her go if she must. He stayed where he was, the wreckage of the day's papers strewn around him. There was no mention of Donnachie in any of them. No lurid stories of a body found on the shores of Coniston Water or speculation about the whereabouts of a man staying at the Lake View Hotel who'd disappeared without paying his bill.

He'd twice ridden up to the hotel, looking in vain for signs of police activity. He'd also taken to buying any evening paper and scanning its columns for the first small hint of trouble. But so far, so good.

Obviously there was no way of knowing how many people committed murder and got away with it but there had to be some. There might even be many.

Then, as he'd almost convinced himself he was home and dry the doubts would begin. Bodies had a way of turning up, didn't they? Popping out years later. And in his case there were two. Not only Donnachie but Senior as well. One under earth; one under water.

Doubling the likelihood of eventual detection. His stomach gave a lurch of fear. He couldn't really get away with it, could he?

And then there was the crime and punishment syndrome. The guilt that grew from itch to all-consuming passion till it could be ended only by his own death.

Well, he knew about that of course. His education hadn't been completely wasted. But somehow he couldn't see it happening to him. Not all that anguish and self-disgust. And, anyway, be fair. He'd acted, not for cash, but in defence of his lover and to stop a wretched blackmailer in his tracks. Neither Senior nor Donnachie had been churchgoing family men; both were professional thugs whose own hands were probably stained with a fair amount of blood.

The pity now was that he couldn't tell Julie and set her at her ease. It would be unfair—and perhaps just a bit unsafe—to burden her with the news that he'd killed Donnachie. He could only sit and watch her go on worrying until she'd gradually come to realise the blackmail had stopped.

Two days later, at Martyn's suggestion, they spent the morning raking up the leaves that'd carpeted the garden and driveway, leaving the trees bare. Behind the bungalow was an unkempt patch that was supposed to be a vegetable garden but that would do now as somewhere to light a fire. It was started with the help of the newspapers Martyn had taken to reading so assiduously, and they stood warming themselves against it.

"What's happened to your committee? The one at the hospital?" asked Martyn, curious as to what she'd say.

"Oh . . . not a lot. I might not go again."

"Why not?"

She gave him a resentful glance—what business was it of his?

"I just might not, that's all."

"OK," he said. "Fine."

"When are you going to go?"

Her question took him by surprise. She wasn't looking at him but at the heap of slowly burning leaves.

"Go? What, you mean leave?"

A little nod of her head said yes, that was what she meant.

"I don't know. Do you want me to?"

She shrugged. "Not particularly."

There was a silence. The truth was he'd shelved all plans for leaving till he discovered whether he'd got away with Donnachie's murder. Illogical, he had to admit. The first urge of most killers was to put as much ground as possible between themselves and the scene of the crime. Yet here he was, hanging around, unwilling to tear himself away.

It was, he realised, a fear that things would start to happen the moment he turned his back. An illusory sense of being in control so long as he stayed on.

"What are you going to do?" he retaliated.

"Me?" she said. "God knows. But something. Oh, don't worry about me. I've got a guardian angel to look after me!"

Her smile didn't have much conviction. She seemed increasingly often to be drawn and desperate with just the odd flash of brittle gaiety as if she were trying to remember and get back to what she'd been like when she'd come wandering up to him on the lake shore. A great deal had changed since his days as an idle boat minder.

"But are you going to stay on here or what?" he insisted.

"I was hoping somebody else could tell me that," she said. He supposed it was a joke. "I could always go back to London and get a job as a model. What do you think? You think I should go back to exposing my tits to the nation?"

"No," he said dully.

"Neither do I."

And that seemed to be that as she went back to gazing into the smouldering leaves.

"I'll go and collect some more," he said, and took the wheelbarrow round to the front of the bungalow where the drive was still to be cleared.

As he came round the corner, his eye was caught by a movement in the lane beyond the gate—a flash of colour and then he
heard the sound of footsteps going away. It might have been
innocent enough, a hiker or neighbour, but then again . . . he
hurried to the gate but his own footsteps carried the alarm before
him. The other person began to run and he caught no more than
a glimpse of a disappearing figure.

He remained there, his heart pounding and his hands tight on
the shaft of the rake. His first impulse had been to charge down
the lane in pursuit but he'd been restrained by the thought of
what'd happened when he'd followed Donnachie. He couldn't
risk another violent confrontation.

Could it have been kids? The glimpsed figure had certainly
been on the short side, but then why the running away? There
was no damage to be seen and not much they could have been
pinching.

He started raking up the leaves, though he now worked
mechanically, his mind elsewhere. Had it been the police? Or
some friend of Donnachie's bent on revenge? As his mind threatened to panic at the implications of either possibility, he could
only clutch at the straw that neither policeman nor mobsters
seemed likely to go careering off down lanes at his approach.
Perhaps it'd been kids after all. Pray God.

He filled the wheelbarrow and returned to the fire.

"I've got to make a phone call," said Julie, who didn't seem to
have moved.

"Yes?"

"And I've been thinking. I might go to London after all. Just
for a while. For a few days."

She seemed to be waiting on his approval.

"OK. When?"

"I don't know. Perhaps at the weekend?" She took a deep
breath and then spoke swiftly as if reciting something she'd been
rehearsing in her mind. "I just think it'd do me good to get away
for a while and to see some people again. And please don't think
it's anything to do with you because it isn't."

He hadn't thought that. Whatever devil she was fighting was in
herself. She still seemed to find comfort in his company and had
surprised him the other night while they were watching TV by

snuggling up to him in an embrace that'd ended with them making love on the lounge floor.

"I think you should go," he said. "Have a good time. Stay for longer if you like. I'll look after this place."

"You're very kind." It was as if she regretted it. "I'm sorry if I've buggered things up for you."

"You haven't," he protested, not sure what she was thinking of. "I mean it's been marvellous. And it still is."

She gave him a grateful smile and then a small, chaste kiss before walking away towards the bungalow.

Martyn tipped the load of leaves onto the fire, then set off to collect more. Remembering what'd happened last time, he left the wheelbarrow at the side of the bungalow, crept stealthily to the corner and peered out.

There was no one there. He strode quickly down the drive and stepped out into the lane but this time there was no flash or sound of movement but for the beating of birds he'd disturbed by his sudden approach.

Despite the revulsion she'd once expressed towards that city, the prospect of a trip to London seemed to raise Julie's spirits. Or perhaps it was the prospect of going anywhere at all, getting away from all those brooding fells and that flat, glassy expanse of water. She went on a small shopping expedition and returned with a pair of fur-lined boots and a long woollen scarf.

"I'm going to drive down," she said, "so I've arranged to have the car serviced. If I take it in, can you give me a lift back on your bike?"

Not since the day she'd given it to him had she been on the pillion of the Suzuki. She seemed to enjoy it, yelling in his ear against the wind and happy to repeat the ride in the evening when they went to collect the serviced Porsche.

"You haven't started backing horses?" she said, looking at him quizzically.

"No," he said, surprised, then realised she was referring to the evening paper he'd been and bought while she was paying for the car.

"Then why have you got your nose in that rag every night?"

"No particular reason."

But something in his manner must have betrayed him for she stepped up to him and said quietly, "You're not still worried about you-know-who that we put you-know-where . . . ?"

"You mean Senior," he muttered.

"Of course I mean bloody Senior."

"Not really, no."

She took it as an admission. "Then don't be. Idiot. That's gone, finished, never happened."

If only you knew, he thought. But he threw the newspaper into a wastepaper bin and got back on the bike.

Perhaps there'd come a time, twenty, twenty-five or thirty years hence, when they'd meet and be able to look back on this summer and think of themselves as different people—so much would they be changed—and he'd at last be able to tell her about how he'd murdered Donnachie. And she'd be surprised and intrigued but not alarmed because it'd seem so long ago, an error of their relative youth for which they'd be no longer answerable.

"I'm going on Saturday," she said. "Staying for a few days."

It was all she told him. He didn't ask about where she'd stay or what she'd do. Nor just how many days were "a few."

The night before she went, they decided to resume something of their old ways and went to the Rockingham for a meal. Martyn had lamb chops and Julie had steak, though she did little more than pick at it, leaving most of it on her plate.

"Madam didn't like the steak?" asked the waiter, almost tearful.

"I love it," said Julie. "So much I couldn't bring myself to eat it."

Unsure about that, he collected the plates and scuttled off.

By the time they got back to the bungalow she'd already had, by Martyn's calculations, the best part of the two bottles of wine they'd supposedly shared, plus a brandy and soda, plus a large whisky. Plus, as a hopeless inadequate antidote, a small black coffee.

"I'm sorry," she said thickly, "but I'm going to bed. Goodnight."

Tucking the whisky bottle under her arm, she picked up a glass, cigarettes, matches and magazine and disappeared into her bedroom. He heard the door close and then—an odd touch—a faint scraping which it took a moment's thought to identify as a bolt being pushed home.

He was more puzzled than offended. He never went to her bedroom unless expressly invited—they'd always kept a certain living distance between them—so why should she now feel the need to bar the door against him?

He watched the late news. It told him about the run-up to the presidential elections in the United States and about political infighting in England. More importantly, it made no mention of bodies being found anywhere north of Watford.

It was nearly lunchtime before she managed to leave and then she still looked ghastly, pale-faced with heavy, bloodshot eyes. Her old ability to throw off a hangover during her first cup of coffee seemed to have deserted her.

"My own fault," she kept saying. "My own bloody fault."

He wouldn't let her go until she'd had some breakfast. It was a long drive for anyone feeling as badly as she looked. He made her egg and bacon from which she turned away, retching.

"But you've got to eat something," he objected.

"Don't tell me what I've got to fucking eat! Who do you think you are anyway, my mother or my nurse or what?"

He went quiet.

Seeing she'd offended him, she said, "Oh, give me some toast. I'll eat some toast."

The other thing she took from the kitchen was money. Lots by the look of it; about half of what was in the drawer, which meant two thousand pounds, give or take the odd hundred.

"I hate being in London without a lot of money," she explained. "It doesn't mean I'll spend it. It's just for luck. Like some people carry a Saint Christopher medal."

When she was finally ready to leave, her actual getaway took him by surprise. He went to open the gates at the foot of the drive, expecting then to walk back to her so they could embrace and say goodbye but, almost before he'd had time to get out of the way, she was driving past him and he had to be content with a wave and a whiff of exhaust fumes.

He went back inside. Strange how her departure, though only seconds old, altered the feel of the place and gave it a vacant, deserted air. It was a relief too—he had to admit that—a relief to be alone again and have time to sort a few things out.

Feeling he had decisions to make and wishing to be methodical, he found a notepad and a ballpoint pen and started to make a list.

Number one had to be housekeeping. The place was a tip. Number two, shopping. That'd always been another of Julie's little weaknesses. Number three, fuel. They needed coal and wood. He'd have to order them in town. Number four . . . well, let's call number four the future. As a large item, it merited a breakdown into subsections. Subsection A, for example, could be jobs—applications for. Subsection B could be relationships—where to now?

There was a knock at the front door. It surprised Martyn, since knocks at the door had been few and far between and usually meant postmen with parcels or milkmen with bills. He put down the notepad and pen, padded in his stocking feet along the hallway and opened the door.

Standing there, practically on the doorstep, were two policemen. They were in uniform but had flat caps rather than helmets. One had a Zapata moustache; the other wore steel-rimmed spectacles. Behind them, their patrol car was parked on the driveway.

"Ah," said Martyn.

If it meant anything, it meant his world had just disintegrated before his eyes; it meant he foresaw in that instant his own public degradation and humiliation, the despair of his parents and the glee of the gutter press.

"Mr. Culley?" said the policeman with the Zapata moustache. Martyn nodded.

"May we have a word?"

He nodded again, then, clearing his throat, said, "Come in." "Thank you."

He turned and walked as if in a trance back into the lounge. Behind him, the two policemen took off their flat caps and followed.

XIX

He led them into the kitchen, where one perched on a stool and the other leaned against the table, his arms folded. It was the one with the Zapata moustache who did the talking.

"You used to work for Mr. Hutton, Mr. Joe Hutton, operating his boats for him?"

"Yes."

It wasn't the question he'd expected; though perhaps they were being clever and approaching things obliquely, via the boats. Which meant it must be Donnachie's body that'd been found.

"And when you worked for Mr. Hutton, didn't he provide a caravan for you to live in?"

"Yes," said Martyn, puzzled. And with the puzzlement came the first gleam of hope.

"But you moved out of the caravan."

"Yes."

"When was that?"

"Oh . . . months ago."

"And what sort of state was it in when you left it?"

He thought of the broken windows and the night of the storm when Julie had turned up to rescue him. Was that what had brought them here?

"It was a mess. The windows had been broken." What more could he say? Anything to help: let them see what a law-abiding character he was. "Then the rain got in. I mean it was pretty uninhabitable." And even, daringly, a little joke: "Which is why I stopped inhabiting it."

"Did you break the windows?"

"Me? No."

"You're sure?"

"Yes."

He wanted to laugh, to dance on the kitchen table, in celebration of his reprieve. It was the caravan they'd come about. Nothing else. It was no more than Joe Hutton after his pound of flesh because he'd at last discovered that somebody had wrecked his wreck of a caravan. Wonderful.

"Do you know who did break the windows?" went on the policeman patiently.

"No idea. It certainly wasn't me. I was supposed to be living in it at the time. I got back late one night and . . . there it was."

"You didn't have any grudge against your employer?"

"No."

"Because he paid you badly? Anything like that."

"No."

The policemen exchanged a look.

"Very well," said Zapata. "Only we had to come and ask you."

"That's all right," said Martyn. Then, curious: "But he must have known before. Those windows have been like that for months now."

The policeman shrugged. "Dunno. Unless it's an insurance job."

"Insurance . . . ?"

"If he's only just got round to claiming on it, and they're insisting he reports it to us first. Anyway we won't keep you any longer."

With one mind they put on their caps. Martyn moved quickly to get ahead of them and open the front door. The one without the moustache lingered and glanced curiously about him as if wondering how Martyn had managed the graduation from a clapped-out caravan to what would be a fairly desirable residence once it was cleaned up. But he said nothing and followed his colleague outside.

The following morning there came another surprise, this time lying on the doormat when he got up rather later than usual. It was a letter from the BBC inviting him to attend for interview.

"Good God," he said aloud.

He was long past expecting job applications to bear fruit. They were simply nudges in the back of the national economy: I'm still here—remember me?

And now, suddenly, here was the BBC being gracious enough to write back and ask could he present himself at Bush House, Portland Place, London, at eleven in the morning in just over two weeks' time. They would pay his expenses (second-class rail fare) and would be grateful for an early reply. And, all right it might not lead to anything careerwise—probably wouldn't—but what it would do—had already done by landing on the doormat—was give him the small push he needed to leave the bungalow, leave Julie to get back on his travels.

It couldn't have come at a better time. Straight after the police visit which, with all its absurdities, had been a watershed for him. That moment he'd found the law on his doorstep and believed the worst to have happened had been a liberating one. His recurring nightmare had for a few seconds become reality and was now behind him. It was to Joe Hutton, the mean old bastard, he owed his freedom.

He sat down and wrote an immediate reply to the interview invitation, saying yes, he'd be attending. Then he put the letter in an envelope and went out there and then, riding into town so he could get it in the post and the decision would be irrevocable.

Two weeks would surely give Julie time to get back so he could tell her of his decision to leave. He didn't want to slope off in her absence, leaving keys under doormats and an empty house. That would smack too much of desertion. He had to see her and tell her face to face of his plans.

There was a small loose end still to be tidied up, too.

After he'd got the house shipshape, he set about the garden. It'd been long neglected and was heavy work but he enjoyed it, finding himself pleasantly tired at the end of each day.

It was on one such day he again became aware of someone in the lane, someone who wasn't just passing the house but had stopped to observe it.

He was clearing the thickly weeded beds beneath the hydrangea bushes that grew to a dense thicket at the side of the bungalow and so was hidden from view—when he heard the footsteps and then, peering through the foliage, caught again a glimpse of colour from the lane. There was someone there. And this time, he was determined, they weren't going to flee before he could get a look at them.

He moved cautiously, staying under cover of the bushes as far as he could. He'd put down the hoe he was using then, too late, wished he'd taken it with him: he didn't know who he was going to confront or what their interest in him might be. As he hesitated, the footsteps began to move away. It was now or never. He burst from the shrubbery and in a few quick strides was at the gate and had a view of the lane and the figure in it.

"Oh . . . !" she cried in surprise.

In his relief he gave an involuntary laugh, then turned it into a welcoming smile, not wanting to betray what his fears had been.

"Wendy," he said. "Hello."

"You gave me a fright."

"I'm sorry."

"I was . . . I was just passing."

"You should have called. How are you?"

"All right."

She was looking past him, so he said, "Julie's not here. She's away for a few days." At which she relaxed her watchful attitude and took a few steps towards him.

"I was just passing," she repeated.

"Look, come in. Come and have a coffee."

"Are you sure?"

"Of course I am. Come on."

It surprised him to find how pleased he was to see her. He'd become too much the hermit these past few days and welcomed the chance of a talk . . . though there was still an awkwardness between them. They might have been lovers, but getting her in for a cup of coffee seemed a more difficult step than getting into her bed.

He left his mud-caked shoes at the door and she followed him in, now unashamedly intrigued by this chance to enter the other woman's property and observe the evidence of her life with Martyn.

He put some coffee on.

"Can I ask you something?"

"What?"

"Have you been here before? A few days ago?" She hesitated so he added with a reassuring smile, "It's just that I thought I saw you but you'd gone before I could say anything."

"Yes," she said, "yes." And then a confession: "I wanted to see you I suppose, but I was afraid she'd be here."

It was another barrier lifted. So it hadn't been one of Donnachie's mates armed with a meat cleaver. Just Wendy Harriman, dewy-eyed and ever hopeful. He felt a rush of gratitude towards her—akin to what he'd felt towards the two policemen—but one to which this time he could give some expression. He pulled her to him and gave her a kiss.

"You don't mind me coming?" she asked, pleased by the show of affection.

"I'm glad you have. I meant to see you but . . . well, things have been difficult."

"Has she gone for good?"

"No," said Martyn, and saw the disappointment in her face. "But I'm going to be leaving soon anyway."

"Really? You're moving out of here?"

"Yes."

The percolator began to make throbbing noises, which meant the coffee was ready. Martyn went to attend to it.

"Where will you be going?"

"London. I've managed to get an interview with the Beeb."

"I'm going to London."

It was said simply but was an offer all the same. To ignore it would leave her high and dry.

"When?" he said.

"Oh, in a week or two. When're you going?"

He smiled. Perhaps after all it was Wendy he needed—into fringe theatre and well out of pornography and murder.

"About the same time by the sound of it. Travel together, shall we?"

"Yes," Then, fearful she was sounding too eager: "I mean I never like hitching on my own. You can get all sorts of weirdos."

Like me, he reflected. If the truth were known, I'd make most of the weirdos look like Duke of Edinburgh Award Winners. But he said nothing. The truth never would be known; he was going to leave it here, behind him.

He poured the coffee. Wendy, looking happier now something had been settled, began to wander round the kitchen.

"It's nice, isn't it, this place. Does it belong to her?"

"I'm not sure. I think it might be the company she works for."

"What sort of company?"

"I'm not sure of that either."

In the end, relenting before her obvious curiosity, he showed her round the bungalow. They stood at the foot of the ladder that climbed to his loft bedroom.

"And you sleep up there?"

"Yes," he said, trying not to catch her eye.

"Can I have a look?"

He nodded and she started up the ladder. Oh well, he thought, why not. Julie was three hundred miles away in the fleshpots of the metropolis. When she got back he was going to tell her of his decision to leave. Morally speaking, he was already a free agent.

And there was Wendy looking down at him from the trapdoor.

"Come on then," she said. "You're not going to leave me up here all alone, are you?"

Julie returned three days later. Which meant she'd been away for a total of eight and left as long again before Martyn was due in London for his interview.

She arrived about seven-thirty in the evening. He was in the middle of his now nightly flip through the local evening paper. Not that he any longer expected to read about bodies, but it'd become a habit that helped to give some sort of pattern to his days. He heard the Porsche approach the house and stop. It was a moment he feared slightly since it heralded some difficult explanations, but it was also a relief: he'd be able to leave in time for his interview after all.

She came in and he moved to meet her. She gave him a hug and a smile, though his first impressions were that she looked drawn and tired.

"How are you? Can I make you some coffee?"

"I'm buggered. And yes, you can."

As he went into the kitchen, he heard the tinkle of glasses from the lounge. She followed him in with a glass of whisky in her hand. He thought again how white and unwell she looked. Though at the same time she carried an air of eagerness and excitement about her.

"I've been on the road for hours. I mean since lunchtime. My backside's aching. God knows why this place has to be so far from anywhere."

"Did you have a good time?"

"What, in London? Not really, no. I'll tell you about it in a minute. Just let me get here first." Then she suddenly pointed at him. "Hey wait. I've got something for you."

She put down her glass and went out to the car, then came back lugging her suitcase.

"I could have brought that," he protested.

"Shut up," she said, opening it on the kitchen table and searching through a jumble of clothes and makeup. "There. With all my love. And just to prove I didn't forget about you altogether."

She gave him a kiss and a small wrapped box which he started to open.

"I'll tell you what it is then you can look delighted when you get to it. It's an electronic chess game. It sort of plays you at chess. Won't play me because I can't play the bloody game to start with, but I was sure you'd be able to."

"Yes, I can," he said. "Thanks. It's great."

"Now tell me about you. What have you been doing?"

"Not a lot."

"You've cleaned up. You've taken advantage of my absence to destroy the charming, pigstye environment I so carefully created, you bum."

He laughed, pleased that her trip at least seemed to have knocked her out of her depression.

"I did the garden, too," he confessed.

"You'll make somebody a lovely husband," she said, then added, "and don't worry, that's not a proposal."

They had the coffee and she told him a little about London—a show she'd seen, the shock of finding herself back there after months away, some amusing incidents. All related with her old cynicism and eye for the ridiculous but, beneath her jibes at the grimy, crisis-ridden metropolis, he detected a real pleasure from having returned to it. And something else, too. That the account he was being given skirted neatly around the edges of what she'd really been about down there. She might have taken in the odd theatre or strolled around the West End as he'd been hearing, but that hadn't absorbed eight days nor sent her back in this hyped-up condition.

"So what have you decided?" she asked suddenly, coming to the end of her stories.

"About what?"

"About what to do. Whether to go or stay. You know damn well about what."

He smiled, admitting that, yes, he did. And then gave the little speech he'd already prepared in his head.

"I heard from the BBC. They want me to go down for an interview next week. So I've said I'll go. Which means I'll probably be away for quite a while. I seem to find it difficult to go back to places once I've left them."

Despite the time he'd had to prepare it, it came out like a pretty transparent and roundabout way of announcing that he was buggering off.

She didn't seem to mind one little bit.

"Perhaps I'll see you there then."

"At the BBC?"

"London, idiot. I've decided I'm not staying here either."

And—the unspoken part of her message—wherever she went, it wasn't going to be with him. It was as amicable a parting of the ways as he could ever have hoped for.

"Now," she said, "you can play with your chess thing. I'm going to unpack and then I've got to have some food."

"When did you last eat?"

"About three days ago. You can carry that through for me if you like."

She meant the suitcase. He followed her with it into the bedroom and put it on the bed. Then, since they were standing together, he put his arms around her.

"Don't say you want to screw a girl who hasn't had a wash or a bite to eat for the last God-knows-how-long."

He stepped away. "No. Sorry." And left her to get on with her unpacking.

Perhaps then she saw their relationship as already over. He felt almost let down by the discovery that there'd be none of the difficult scenes for which he'd prepared himself. Still, count your blessings.

She didn't want to go out to eat. "I want to eat in. I've come back all this way to eat in. If I'd wanted to eat out, I'd have stayed there. Why don't we get a Chinese takeaway?"

"All right," he said, knowing it'd be no use arguing. "I'll go."

She'd washed her hair and turbaned it in a towel. She was wearing a dressing gown and nothing on her feet. Now she perched on her haunches before the fire and gave him her order. "Chicken chow mein and fried rice. And a banana fritter."

"Chicken chow mein. Fried rice. Banana fritter," he repeated.

"And when you come back . . ." She stopped, but smiled and nodded as if in confirmation of some secret they shared.

"What?"

"I've got some things to tell you. Things I want you to know."

He hovered in the doorway, suddenly unwilling to leave without being more certain of what he'd be coming back to.

"Tell me about what?"

"About everything. About what I did in London. And why. And about a lie I once told you."

Of all the tidbits offered, it was the last one he caught at.

"What lie?"

She only nodded. "I'll tell you. I promise I'll tell you."

Her nervous excitement communicated itself to him, making him uneasy. What lie was this? And where would knowing the truth leave him? The sooner he went, the sooner he'd find out.

"I'll see you later then," he said.

Once sure he'd gone, she brought a toilet bag from the bedroom and took out and arranged its contents on the coffee table before her. There were a number of plastic syringes and needles, a piece of rubber tubing, a bottle of surgical spirit, cotton wool, a bottle of sterile water, and some twists of paper, each containing 15 milligrammes of heroin in powdered form.

She opened one of the twists of paper and added a half teaspoonful of the sterile water to its contents, fitted a needle to a syringe and drew up the mixture into it. This she then placed to one side.

Next she applied the rubber tubing as a tourniquet around the top of her left arm, all the while moving the fingers of her left hand in a pumping action. She then cleaned an area of her forearm with surgical spirit, selected a now enlarged vein and speared it with the needle. Withdrawing the plunger slightly to check her aim, she was rewarded by the sight of her own blood sucking back into the syringe.

It'd been a practised, step-by-step operation, the final stage of which was to exert the slow pressure that pushed the heroin into her body.

XX

Every year as the days got shorter and the sunset came earlier, Ezra Joseph's Friday evenings became more of a problem. He had to be at the Beavis Marks synagogue on Whitechapel Road in time to bring in shabbas; yet Friday was his busiest day at the bakery with the ovens churning out the challah loaves his customers demanded; and, as an orthodox Jew, he was forbidden to use his car to take him the distance from Stepney to Whitechapel.

When he was younger he'd been able to make it—just—at a fast run or walk. Since his fiftieth birthday and his first attack of angina he'd decided the Lord was surely more concerned he should arrive at all than with the manner of that arrival. So now he took his car and drove—but took care to park out of sight of his fellow worshippers, usually on an area of derelict land a couple of blocks away from the synagogue.

On this particular Friday evening he'd checked the doors were locked and the windows closed, then hurried off, carrying with him a small royal blue velvet bag on which a *mogen Dovid* was embroidered in gold. The bag contained his white prayer shawl, his *tefela*, with its leather straps folded in the approved fashion, his white *capul* and his *l'moidik*. The car was a powder-blue Volvo estate.

When Mal Croxley had spotted it twenty minutes later, he couldn't believe his luck. An expensive motor that wouldn't look out of place where he was going, and so helpfully parked, away from prying eyes and streetlights. He'd approached cautiously. Surely there had to be a catch? Perhaps a sleeping alsatian on the backseat? When he saw there wasn't, it'd taken him a little under a minute and a half to force a window, then another thirty seconds to start the engine.

He might even have been quicker but for the gloves he was

wearing—thin cotton ones that did little to keep out the cold but kept him from leaving his prints on everything he touched.

His unexpected find had put him ahead of schedule and he could drive slowly. The first traffic lights he approached were at amber; rather than jumping them, he stopped.

A passerby looking into the waiting car would have seen a young man with ginger hair and a moustache; the streetlights at the junction might even have picked out the line of an old scar by his left eye.

What they certainly couldn't have shown was the Luger pistol which weighed heavily in the right-hand pocket of his jacket and which he'd bought earlier that day from a one-eyed Polish dealer in King's Cross for ninety-five pounds that'd included six rounds of ammunition and a guarantee of sorts.

"It might be old," the dealer had said, "but it'll work. My life on it."

"Your life's already on it," Mal Croxley had replied, handing over the money.

And now the evening found him, all tooled up, with a nice motor that might have been left specially for him, driving like a maiden aunt towards number 17, Blackhorse Road, Richmond.

They ate in the lounge, straight from the foil containers. Martyn waited patiently until, after a few mouthfuls of chicken chow mein, Julie at last began the account he'd been promised.

"I said I'd got something to tell you?"

"Yes."

"I hope you won't hate me for it." She waited for reassurance. He did the best he could. "I'll try not to."

"Only, see, I lied to you about something. And, before you go off to London or wherever it is so that perhaps I won't see you again, I want to tell you what it was."

He shrugged: OK, so tell me.

"You know that when I was living in London—before I ever came up here—you know I was involved with . . . vice." And she gave a little self-conscious giggle at the terminology.

"Yes."

"But I didn't go into details."

"No, you didn't." Nor had he wanted her to.

"Well, I was the girlfriend, and then the sort of partner—I mean in the business sense a partner as well as in the other sense —of one of the organisers. He was called Arnie Bish. And, boy, did I work hard to get that partnership. I mean I couldn't offer shorthand and typing so . . ."

"I can imagine," he said, cutting her short.

"During this last summer there was a lot of aggro between Arnie and another . . . well, whatever you want to call 'em. Another gangster—I suppose you'd call 'em gangsters . . . ?"

"I suppose you might."

"He's called Donald Maloney. There was a lot of aggro between Arnie and him. God knows why. These things always sort of grow out of nothing, which is why nobody knows how to stop them when once they get started."

Martyn's feeling of disquiet had begun to focus itself. "Is this to do with Senior?"

She looked at him with wide, staring eyes. "What?"

"Senior," he said, becoming almost irritable in his wish to pin her down. "The man you . . . the man we buried."

She made a gesture, putting up both hands before her face. It said: don't crowd me. Let me tell it in my own way.

"All right," he said. "Go on."

"There was all this aggro," she repeated. "During the summer."

"Between Arnie Bish and Donald Maloney."

"Yes. There was a lot of property smashed up and some people got hurt."

Like Senior, he thought. Hurt beyond recovery and buried in a not-so-shallow grave with a stream running over it. But he said nothing. Gnawed at a sparerib.

"Anyway, the Old Bill . . . that's the police . . ."

"I know."

"The police started to lean on everybody and so things calmed down. Or seemed to calm down. Calmed down on the surface."

She suddenly gave a grimace of distaste, leaned over and dropped her container of food into the wastebin.

"I hate this muck," she said, and wiped her hands and mouth on a tissue.

"Do you want anything else?" asked Martyn patiently.

"No," she said, and went to get herself a whisky.

He waited but she said nothing, concentrating on pouring herself a drink—and, God, what a drink it was, nearly a glassful—then lighting a cigarette. He was about to prompt her with a question about Bish or Maloney when she suddenly came back on stream.

"Course I'd got out of it. Well, I thought I'd got out of it. But then what you find is that you can't. Well, not—I mean let's be honest, not if you keep taking the bloody money. Can't get out of it then."

Bloody money indeed, that they still had stacks of, in the kitchen drawer below the cutlery.

"Even so," she said, "I thought I'd got away, that I'd really managed it. I mean it's a long way from here to London. A bloody long way."

"You got out when you found your friend was on heroin," he said.

"What?"

"Your friend was on heroin. Wasn't she?"

"Oh yes. Yes, she was. And she died. Yes."

He had the distinct impression that, until he'd reminded her, the poor dead friend had been all but forgotten about.

"Julie," he said quietly, "is this all to do with Senior? Is there something about him you want to tell me?"

"Senior . . . ?"

"The man who came up here and . . . and threatened you."

She nodded slowly, thoughtfully. "I suppose it is, yes."

"Has anybody found out? I mean found out what happened to him?"

She looked at him. Gave a faint almost pitying smile and shook her head.

"But it didn't."

"What?"

"It didn't happen to him. Not like you think."

Blackhorse Road was an avenue of detached houses, all highly desirable stuff with the Thames a stone's throw away and all the people—blacks, yobboes—who habitually threw stones a good deal further.

Croxley, arriving in his powder-blue Volvo, at first had been able to park no nearer than thirty yards or so from number 17 where his intended victim lived but then, waiting patiently until other cars departed, he'd managed to move up into the ideal spot right by the gate itself. He could now see up the short drive to the house. It was a red brick, prewar house with double bay windows and three steps up to the solid-looking front door. There were lights on in most of the downstairs rooms, all of which had their curtains closed. There was also a light outside the kitchen door, which was useful. It illuminated the area to the side of the house where a silver-grey Audi stood in front of the garage. The distance from the kitchen door to the car was about ten yards.

Croxley knew that his own car—the one he'd nicked—by now would almost certainly have been reported to the police as stolen. Any cruising cop car might spot the number and he'd suddenly have a lot of explaining to do, explaining that wouldn't be made any easier by the Luger in his right-hand pocket.

Not that he cared. It wasn't only that the cruising cop cars were unlikely in that neighbourhood: he had an unshakable faith in his own good fortune. Nobody had yet put a hand on his collar or come near to it. It was as if he'd come to a working arrangement with the law: he ignored them and they ignored him.

It wasn't clever planning or that he covered his tracks brilliantly. Just that he didn't mess about; went in and did it and then go out again. He distrusted meticulous stratagems, preferring to react instinctively to whatever the moment offered.

Like tonight. His opportunity would come somewhere in that ten yards between house and car. Then it'd all be down to speed and resolution.

No, sitting in a stolen car was no sweat.

His gloved hand went to his pocket as the kitchen door opened. For a moment no one appeared. Then, when someone eventually did, it was a woman. A rather plump, homely-looking woman, aged about forty. She bent and there was a clink of glass. She was putting out the milk bottles.

Might as well make it one pint less for tomorrow, he thought.

She went back in, the door was closed and he settled back to waiting again, though left restless and on edge for a while by the spray of adrenalin that'd leapt around his body when he'd thought the moment had come.

He fiddled with the car radio, moving from station to station, catching bits of music and then, turning the knob more quickly, running them together into a sort musical omelette. There was a cassette player too but the cassettes in the glove compartment were all classical with the single exception of Nana Mouscouri whom he didn't fancy either.

A moment later he was filled with dismay. "Shit," he said, and snapped the radio off with such force the knob came off in his hand.

A car had pulled across the front of him, into the driveway of number 17. It was a Mercedes, though more than that he couldn't see in the gloom. A man got out of the driver's seat and slammed the door shut.

The man was so fat that he waddled rather than walked forward into the area of light around the kitchen door. It was his shape rather than his features that identified him to Croxley as Max Zabadak, a lawyer who specialised in representing villains.

As Zabadak was admitted to the house, Croxley consoled himself with the thought that at least it hadn't been a minder, who might have been on his guard and caused complications. Zabadak was unlikely to do more than piss himself; if he retained any presence of mind it'd be to give Croxley his card in case he ever needed representation.

Perhaps Zabadak's car was likely to cause more problems than that man himself. There were now two cars in the driveway, the Audi and the Mercedes in front of it. Would they go together to the first or each to his own?

So don't think about it, Croxley told himself. When the time comes it'll happen. The magic that'd always carried him through would do so again.

Martyn waited for her to elaborate on her explosive statement— "It didn't happen to him. Not like you think."—but she said nothing. Instead, she seemed to retreat even further into herself, sitting cross-legged on the floor, arms wrapped tightly around her and eyes fixed on some distant prospect he couldn't share.

In the end he had to ask.

"What didn't happen to him?"

She came alive, took a sip of her drink and looked up.

"What you think."

"I think we took the body out and buried it. In fact, I know we did."

"You think I killed him."

The jolt that gave him was like a physical blow.

"And you didn't?"

"No."

"You mean you didn't stick that kitchen knife into him?"

"I didn't, no."

He wanted to give up, surrender. Admit it was all beyond him and he wanted out. However, being so far in—up to his neck—he had to go on.

"So who did?"

She made him wait while she lit another cigarette.

"About two years ago," she said eventually, "when I was in London, working with Arnie . . ." Then: "Did I tell you I worked with Arnie?"

"At least three times."

"Yes, well . . . my brother, who's a lot younger than I am, wanted a job and came and asked me could I help him and I said no, that I wouldn't, but he came back again and . . . well, I mean I could only say no so many times and then I said yes and asked Arnie if he could find anything for him."

"What's this got to do with Senior?"

"I'm telling you. If you'll just listen, I'm telling you."

"Sorry."

"Anyway, he ended up working for Arnie. My brother did. He ran a shop, he ran a club, he . . . well, he worked for him. And even when I left, when I came up here, he still worked for him."

"Yes."

"Then in the summer, last summer, there was a lot of aggro. God knows how it started . . ."

"You told me."

"I did?"

"Yes."

"Oh, all right then. Well, my brother was involved in that. I mean he was working for Arnie, and so I suppose he couldn't help but be involved in it."

"What happened with Senior?" asked Martyn again.

She ignored him. Continued as if he hadn't spoken.

"Arnie used him to do a job. It was something to do with breaking up a pub I think, I don't know, and so he had to stay out of the way for a while. So he came up here. Came up to see me for a few days." She turned to look at Martyn. "It was when you'd gone down to see your parents."

"I see," he said. As, for the first time, he began to.

"So that my brother was here when Senior came. I mean thank God, thank God he was here . . ." Her voice tailed off and she ended almost tearfully, "to protect me."

"It was your brother who killed Senior," he said flatly.

"Yes." Her brow furrowed with doubt, as if she were realising for the first time that learning he'd been duped into helping dispose of a body might not be his idea of a joke. "I'm sorry. I mean that I lied to you."

He gave a little shrug, not yet sure what he was feeling or wanted to say.

"We'd been out for a drink," she said. "It was lunchtime or after that when we got back, and I was in the kitchen and my brother was . . . well, I don't know where he was but then suddenly there was Senior. He'd let himself in, just walked in, and started mouthing off at me about Arnie and what he was going to do to me and I shouted—No, please, go away. And then my brother came in behind him. It was . . . well, it was almost funny —it would have been funny—to see him look round and see my brother there behind him. He just looked so sick. I almost felt sorry for him. I did. I almost felt sorry for him."

"Who had the knife?"

"Well, nobody. It was on the draining board. My brother picked it up. He said afterwards . . . he swore that he only meant to threaten him with it but . . . well, Senior moved towards him and the next thing I saw the knife was in him. They didn't say anything. Neither of them. Not one word."

She nodded emphatically as if this had been the most amazing aspect of the whole business. How quiet the killing had been.

"And then I arrived," he said, thinking of his bike roaring up the lane and imagining their hearing it and the small panic it must have caused.

"Yes. Well, not long afterwards anyway. We heard the bike coming and I said leave it, it's all right and . . . then you arrived, yes."

Neither had to spell out why she'd then lied and claimed it was she, and not her brother, who'd killed Senior. They'd needed Martyn's collaboration: it'd been a question of how best to get it.

"Where did your brother go?" he asked. Might as well have the full story.

"He let himself out at the back while you were coming in at the front. Then walked back into town."

As easily as that. Well yes, what with the shock of finding the corpse on the kitchen floor, an army of heavy-footed murderers could have marched past without his noticing.

"Leaving us to clear up the mess."

"Sorry," she said again.

He gave a small, helpless laugh.

She waited a moment, then said, "He went back to London."

"Who did?"

"My brother. I asked him not to. I wanted him to get out, to stop working for Arnie Bish."

"Yes?"

"Only he didn't." She started to weep. "They killed him. He didn't get out and they killed him."

This new twist to the tale left him floundering. "Somebody killed your brother . . . ?"

"Not somebody. Maloney did. Donald fucking Maloney. Or one of his . . ." Her face was streaked with tears and she became incoherent for a moment, then wiped a hand across her eyes, took another gulp of her whisky and said, "All I knew was that my brother had disappeared. Nobody knew where he was. Nobody'd seen him."

So that was why she'd seemed so strange and far away. And presumably what her trip to London had been all about. He was sorry to see her grief, though it was relief to hear of a new killing in which he couldn't possibly have been involved.

"How do you know?" he asked. "I mean how can you be sure

he's been killed. Might he not just have taken your advice and got out?"

"No." She was adamant.

"But surely . . ."

"It's the way they work. My brother was working for Arnie. Senior was working for Maloney. My brother killed Senior. So Maloney had him killed. It's the stupid, bloody way they work!"

He could only nod.

She took a swig of her whisky and said, "So it's the way I'm working, too."

"What?"

"It's the way I'm working, too," she repeated, and gave a bitter little smile as though to say: work that one out for yourself.

He did. "You mean you're going to avenge your brother?"

"Exactly."

"How?"

"You don't want to know. You're better off not knowing."

"Please, Julie," he urged. "I don't want you doing anything stupid."

"Oh not *me*," she said. "I mean not me personally. I've . . . hired somebody." And then slowly, as if she couldn't resist hearing it said aloud: "Somebody to kill Maloney for me."

"Oh God," he moaned softly.

"It's all right," she said, misunderstanding his general despair at the state of things with a particular concern for her. "There's no connection with me. It's somebody who . . . who does this sort of thing. It's what you might call a contract. He does it, I pay him, and then it'll all be over."

"It won't bring your brother back," he objected weakly.

"I know." There was a silence, then she muttered, as much to herself as anything, "Half brother."

"What?"

"He was my half brother. I always said brother but he was actually my half brother. My mother married again. We didn't even share the same name."

It was as if the room around them had dissolved, and they were on an open plain over which dark and dreadful forces threatened.

A whisper was the most Martyn could manage.

"What was his name?"

"Whose name?"

"Your . . . your stepbrother's."

"Adrian. Adrian Donnachie," she said. "Why?"

By nine o'clock Croxley was stiff and cold from his long wait in the front seat of the car but undeterred. He'd sit there for twenty-four hours if necessary. What he wasn't going to do was miss that single moment when he'd have to move—and quickly—if he was ever going to collect the balance of a further five thousand that she'd promised him.

In any event, the downstairs lights inside gave him ample warning. The bay windows went suddenly dark, the kitchen lit up, and there was the front door opening at last. The unmistakable bulk of Zabadak emerged first, then came the smaller figure of Donald Maloney, wrapped up against the cold and shouting back farewells over his shoulder.

Croxley was out of the car, walking swiftly up the drive. The sudden movement might well have been agony to his cramped muscles—he wasn't aware. All he knew was the feel of the Luger in his pocket and the two figures ahead of him who'd now noticed his approach but weren't yet alarmed by it.

He went right up to Maloney, so close he saw the fear jump into the man's features, pulled out the Luger and fired twice into his chest. The retorts were deafening and the recoil made his whole arm jump.

Maloney gave a gasp, clutched at himself and fell over.

Croxley put the gun back in his pocket. A voice was saying, as though reciting a prayer, "I've seen nothing. I've seen nothing . . ." and he saw Zabadak standing with his eyes closed. He thought about shooting him but it seemed to matter so little whether he did or didn't that he couldn't decide. There was a scream from inside the house. "I've seen nothing, I've seen nothing . . ." intoned Zabadak. In the end Croxley nearly shot him just to shut him up but now there was a small commotion going on inside the house and, deciding he'd outstayed his welcome, he walked briskly away down the drive.

The car could stay where it was. Without the key it'd take too long to start and, besides, he felt safer and less conspicuous on foot. He came to the end of Blackhorse Road, having passed nobody, and turned towards the tube station. The Luger could be disposed of later or even kept for another occasion.

She was staring at him, puzzled by the change in his manner, the way he'd gripped the arms of his chair and let the remains of his meal, foil container and all, slide from his knees and on to the carpet.

"Donnachie . . . ?" he muttered.

"Yes. Adrian Donnachie."

He shook his head. Couldn't believe it. Wouldn't believe it. There had to be other bits of the story that didn't fit.

"Did he—your younger brother—did he come up here to see you?"

"Yes."

"I mean after he'd killed Senior."

"Yes. Twice. I was trying to talk him into going to America or somewhere. I even gave him some money."

"Was this—the second time—was it when you said you had a meeting at the hospital?"

"Oh, that. Yes. Yes, that was just an excuse. I'm sorry."

"The man you saw that night was your brother . . . ?"

"Yes."

He didn't know who to feel most sorry for, himself, or her, since at least he knew what she didn't.

"I killed him," he said.

"What?" she asked, sure she'd misheard.

"I killed your brother."

She gave a little hesitant laugh as if afraid there was a joke somewhere she was missing out on.

"I thought he was somebody from London blackmailing you and so I killed him."

Perhaps it was the expression on his face that convinced her. Or a faint memory of the argument they'd had about money she'd taken from the kitchen drawer and given to Donnachie when the idea of blackmail had been hinted at. Anyhow, she didn't protest or try and argue. Just stared, as if seeing him for the first time.

"How?" she said finally.

"How?"

"How did you kill him?"

Avoiding her gaze, he gave a muttered account of how he hit him on the head and dropped him into the lake.

"When?"

"The night that you last saw him. I followed him after you'd dropped him at the hotel."

She began to rant. "You stupid bastard. You stupid, murderous bastard . . ." until the words lost all sense and became a jumble of obscenities. She got up and swept the mantelpiece of its few ornaments and threw her glass past his head to smash against the wall. She rushed from the room, then, not knowing where she was going, came back in again and had another go at him, shouting and screaming.

Martyn didn't move. Only his shallow breathing and the movement of his eyes as they followed her betrayed he was even conscious. If his confession had sent her off into paroxysms of fury, it'd left him stunned and, quite simply, with nothing more to say. Feeling he'd never have anything more to say again.

She finished shouting and stood panting and moaning. Till something occurred to her.

"Oh God," she said. "Oh no."

She hurried from the room, then came back, holding her diary.

"I've got to catch him," she said.

"Who?" murmured Martyn.

But she didn't answer. Instead, she began to dial, reading the number from the diary she was holding. It was a London number. She finished dialling and waited.

"Oh, come on," she said. "Please. Come on."

The phone rang and rang inside the seventh-floor council flat but there was no one to answer it, only the neighbours on either side to curse the idiocy of whoever couldn't take no for an answer—till it did finally stop and the flat, with its shabby furniture and its view of the Mile End Road, was silent again.

Elsewhere, though, things were far from silent. The commander of West End Central had been dragged from a Masonic Lodge meeting to be told Donald Maloney had been shot outside his house. His first reaction was to get Chief Superintendent Forsyth on the phone and give him an earful before hurrying into his office.

The news of Maloney's killing had already spread through Soho so that police and villains alike were at battle stations, condition red alert. There was a feeling of expectation and fear, almost tangible in the pubs and clubs and running like a thin current through the streets.

It was almost like old times.

XXI

It wasn't a bad turnout considering shift patterns and the fact that most of his old colleagues had retired, died or gone to work for Securicor. There was a sprinkling of top brass, all of his present squad and a few old-timers in civvies. They sat around the tables of the recreation room while the commander addressed them.

". . . It was in 1954 that Constable John Forsyth, as he was then, began to pound the beat with probably little idea of what the next thirty years were to hold for him. If he had known, would he have done things differently? Well, from my association with Chief Superintendent Forsyth, as he is now, I would say not . . ."

For once Johnny Forsyth, sitting beside the commander, silently agreed with his superior officer. Perhaps it was just the sentimentality of the occasion, or the glasses of wine he'd had before it, but, no, he wouldn't have swopped a minute of it for a different job. Police work was all he knew or had ever wanted to know. Even though he was now leaving of his own accord, it was a painful wrench and he'd be glad when it was over.

He could have done without the grand finale of course. He'd been counting on a quiet exit, proof of a job well done, until Maloney had gone and got himself murdered outside his own front door and all of a sudden no one knew what was going to happen next and whether all hell was going to be let loose or just a bit of it.

He'd had Arnie Bish picked up that same night. Of course he had a rock-hard alibi—these buggers had alibis like other people had clothes, kept on hangers for suitable occasions—and he'd protested his innocence with all the passion of the professional criminal.

"Why should I want him dead? He was a friend of mine!"

"A friend? Really? Your trouble is you don't know the meaning of the word."

"Oh, we've had our disagreements . . ."

"You can say that again."

"But them was over. I mean, Mr. Forsyth, please, you know better than anybody that them was over."

"They are now."

"They already were. 'Cause you made sure they were, right? You had me in here. I listened to you. You told me if there was any more bother then I was for the high jump. I listened to what you said!"

"Did you."

"On my mother's grave, Mr. Forsyth."

"Why is it I don't believe a word you say?"

"I don't know. I don't honestly."

"I told you I wasn't having any more of it, right?"

"Right."

"And that if you put one foot out of line then I'd do everything I could to get you stopped once and for all. Regardless of where the manure might fly when once it'd hit the fan."

"But I'm innocent, Mr. Forsyth."

"So was Timothy Evans. And look what happened to him."

Even so, it hadn't been an easy decision. Bish had thought himself untouchable because of the leeway he'd been given by Johnny Forsyth's predecessor and for which he'd paid handsomely. If Bish were to be brought to book and his little empire shut down there'd have to be some dredging through pretty murky waters to find the evidence that'd do it. It went against the grain to be leaving a mess behind him for somebody else to clear up.

But he'd done it all the same. Submitted a full report on Bish with no punches pulled. He'd had to. Either that or let Bish get away with . . . well, with murder as like as not.

And the commander would be pleased, he thought. These new get-up-and-go boys all took a secret delight in anything that confirmed their own superiority to the old breed of lovable but corruptible coppers.

Forsyth stood as the commander came to the end of his speech. They were presenting him with a set of crystal and a silver tray on which the details of his career were engraved for posterity and to put anybody off the idea of nicking it.

There was a genuine warmth to the applause as the presentation was made, then the commander sat down and it was Forsyth's turn to speak.

"Commander, ladies and gentlemen," he said. "I won't keep you long because if there's one thing for sure in this job it's that life out there hasn't stopped while we have our little do in here. The stuff that goes on out there, it went on for a hell of a long time before I ever became a bobby and I daresay it'll go on for quite a while to come . . ."

Even as he spoke, he had a vision of the surrounding streets with their pimps and tarts and wandering punters. It was the usual pathetic stew of carnality and commerce, yet for once it suggested an enduring vitality he found almost touching.

Sister Veronica accompanied Martyn past the statue of Our Lady of Perpetual Succour, along the green corridor and into the small private room where Julie was lying propped up in bed and wearing a white nightgown. Her face above it was white and haggard-looking, what with the effects of the drugs and the absence of her customary makeup.

"I'm going," he said, when once Sister Veronica had left them alone. "I have the interview tomorrow so . . . can't leave it any longer."

"Have a good trip," she said. There was just a hint of irony.

"How are you?"

"At the moment, fine. 'Cause I've just had my methadone, see. Thirty mils. Four times a day. They like to give us a dose just before we have any visitors, then we don't upset you too much."

He remembered their conversation in the restaurant when she'd outlined the awful process that took an addict first from heroin onto methadone and then—hopefully, painfully—from methadone to nothing.

"You're looking better," he lied.

"Then you need your eyes tested."

He decided not to argue. "I've locked up the bungalow. And I've given the key to Sister Veronica. I've also given her the rest of the money that was left in the drawer."

"You think we can trust her?" she said.

He laughed, but then was stopped by her sudden command: "Go on. You'd better go."

"I've only just come," he objected.

"I don't want you feeling you have to make promises about coming back and all that crap. Just go." And, when he still resisted, she threatened, "I'll scream my head off and tell Sister Veronica you're trying to screw me. Now get out."

So he kissed her and went, saying nothing about when he'd see her again or telephone or write, though intending to do all three. Their romance was as dead as a dodo—if romance it'd ever been—but they were still friends, and he cared what would happen to her.

Besides which, they'd be forever united by the murders that lay in both their pasts—a stronger bond than any love.

He talked again to Sister Veronica before going out to join Wendy, who was waiting patiently beside the Suzuki in front of the hospital.

"She's got a good deal of spirit," observed the nun. "That can be as important as anything. Though, of course, it's bound to be more difficult this time than it was the last."

He knew already—had guessed before he'd been told—that this was Julie's second stint in the hospital and that there'd been no poor dead friend whom Julie had known, but that it'd been she herself who'd come for treatment. Which was why she'd stayed on in the bungalow in lonely exile, away from the city and among all those lakes and mountains.

Sister Veronica had explained. "Patients often develop an emotional attachment to the hospital where they've been treated. They don't feel secure unless they keep in touch. So, even when the treatment's completed, they often find it difficult to move away and resume their normal lives."

Julie had clung on until, unwittingly, he'd dislodged her, killing her brother and sending her back to the drug pushers she couldn't resist.

"From what she's told me," said Sister Veronica, "I gather she's had a rather colourful past."

"I think so," agreed Martyn, feeling how easy it must be to

confess everything to this serene figure in white and smelling of antiseptic.

"Fortunately God in his wisdom made the past to be unreachable. Otherwise we'd spend all our time trying to alter it."

"Yes," he said in wholehearted agreement.

"The thing is to accept it and move on. Not arrogantly but with humility. Knowing the limits of what we can achieve. And that the past is gone for good."

"Thank you, Sister," he said, taking her hand in farewell.

And wondering suddenly how much Julie had told her. There was something in the look she gave him that made him realise her advice was intended more for himself than for the patient he'd come to visit.

Elkie Brooks was singing "Warm and Tender Love" as the girl on the club's dance floor let the last of her flimsy garments slide off her. It was Johnny Forsyth's second retirement celebration of the day, the unofficial one organised by a few of his old mates and taking place in one of Soho's plushier establishments.

Forsyth, though, was beyond taking much more than a polite interest in the girl's brown limbs: a lifetime of overseeing the sexual habits of his fellow men, followed by a day of continuous drinking, had dulled his appetite. He'd have another brandy, then go while he could still walk. Go for good. Spend time in his garden. Travel a bit. Get that blessed caravan moving at last—if it hadn't rusted solid. Have to wait for the spring now of course.

The girl was writhing around on the floor. He lit a cigarette. The Lakes. He'd go up there, do some walking, fishing even. He hadn't had a rod in his hands since he was a lad but then he might get beginner's luck and land the catch of the season.

PETER WHALLEY began his working life as a teacher, but after ten years he became a free-lance scriptwriter. He has written several radio plays, novels, and numerous episodes of popular television programmes. Currently, he is also working on a new stage thriller. He lives in Lancaster, England, where he was born. *Love and Murder* is his second novel for the Crime Club.